Off-Key
ORCHESTRATION

A Maximo Morgan Mystery

MAY

Copyright 2025 by William LeRoy

All rights reserved. Published by Mossik Press.

mossikpress@mail.com

Library of Congress Cataloguing-in-Publication Data

LeRoy, William [6.10.2025]

Off-Key Orchestration / Cat In The Cradle
by William LeRoy.

p. cm
ISBN 979-8-9992429-0-7

1. Humor—Fiction.
2. Oklahoma, United States—Fiction.
3. Mystery—Fiction.
4. Noir—Fiction.
I. Title

10 9 8 7 6 5 4 3 2 1

Manufactured in the United States of America
First Edition

Off-Key
ORCHESTRATION

A Maximo Morgan Mystery

MAY

WILLIAM LEROY

CHAPTER ONE

At his desk inside a Mister Quickie copy shop workstation cubicle, Max grappled with yet another locked-box mystery.

Yesterday, he had grappled for hours before borrowing Quickie's blower to call a so-called help line. Turned out that his own date of birth—03-16-75 minus 1—was the new so-called password assigned by his phone service provider. Now the telephone company joker was again on the line, but...

With a sigh, Max ended the call for help and gave up trying to dope out how a carelessly placed something-or-other inside a drawer had stuck the sliding box in its desk slot. Quickie would have to call in a carpenter. Copy shop customers and others in and around his Henryetta, Oklahoma stamping ground would have to call the so-called Rotary Notary for curbside service. In the meantime...

Uh oh, into the cubicle came the town's pudgy, baldheaded Mayor, Buford "Booster" Bailey, looking more agitated and red in his round face than usual.

"Sorry, Mayor, the Notary stamper is, uh, out of commission. Come back in a day or two and..."

"I'm here on more important business," said Bailey, dropping into the client chair. "There's a big Fun-'n'-Game charity event tonight, and against my strong objection...Anyway, for some reason an anonymous donor insists that you, the town's only 'private detective', take part in the, uh, entertainment."

Entertainment?

"A so-called escape-room game," said His so-called Honor. "Popular fad in big cities, they say. A group of people go into a themed room — there's one in Oklahoma City called '221 Baker Street' for some reason — and try to figure out clues for how to get out."

Max's ears perked up. 221 Baker Street was the address of the London, England digs of Sherlock Holmes and the famous British detective's case report jotter, Dr. Watson. But...

"You'll be part of a team, locked in, uh, a room during a gala dinner dance, and..."

Uh oh again. In his own recent *Case of Locked in the Loo*, he'd had to cope with a tricky British-style wrong-side flush handle.

"... an anonymous donor has pledged a double-matching gift of $5,000 if a team of players are able to escape from the, uh, room before gala music and dancing begins."

Five thousand clams! A bigly lay, but...Dang it, through bathroom burglars and other wrong numbers always made careless mistakes, sometimes even savvy private dicks, such as Percy Wilson in *Case of That's Not My Wife*...

"Sorry again, Mayor, Yours Truly has come down with a case of what they call closetrophobia."

"Yeah, whatever. I've already talked to Quickie, so if you want to keep stamping Town Hall documents, be at the old Pioneer Bank Building by six-'o-clock sharp..."

The old bank building had been boarded up for years.

"...and to fill-out a roster of six players, bring along a ...Get your mom to be your 'date'," said His Honor, before getting up from the client chair and out of the semi-enclosed cubicle.

Hmmm.

Max had studied all the pulp reports and film documentaries of cases handled by Mike Hammer, Phillip Marlowe, Sam Spade and almost all the other famous gumshoes back in the days and murky nights of *Noir* — with particular focus on those doped out by his role model, Brad Runyon, a/k/a The Fat Man — but as for the Sherlock Holmes so-called Adventures...

Right on cue, the high school kid who served as his own Doc Watson ankled into the cubicle and plopped his over-sized rear end into the client chair. He put the teenaged case report jotter and wannabe P.I. wise to the escape-room lay and…

"Been there, done that," said the smart-alecky kid, a protege of sorts, wide in the beam but with still a lot of listening-and-learning to do before ever sitting in a Fat Man's double-wide chair. "Uncle Ralph—a rabbi and a Sherlockian scholar—took the family to the 221 B Baker Street escape room in OKC.

"Ha! All we had to do was solve an orchestrated case in which, supposedly, Mr. Sherlock had disappeared and was suspected of murdering a newspaper reporter."

"Musical murrrderrr case?"

"Orchestrated in the sense of being a situation set up—usually surreptitiously in cases of murrrderrr—to produce a desired effect. But in the case of the OKC escape-room game, heck, just another commercial pastiche that we saw through in fifteen minutes."

"Pastiche?"

"Imitation of a Holmes case report, Mr. Max. According to Uncle Ralph, the fakery and mockery of Mr. Sherlock adventures started getting popular in the 1970s and 1980s. For crying out loud, one 'mocumentary' was titled *The Adventures of Sherlock Holmes' Smarter Brother*. Another one, titled *The Seven-Per-Cent Solution*, imagined that Mr. Sherlock got treated for cocaine addiction by Dr. Sigmund Freud."

Hmmm.

"Other pastiches were more realistic and believable," the kid continued. "The one titled *Without a Clue* reported that Mr. Sherlock was a brainless bungler, and that Dr. Watson actually solved all their cases. Another—*Sherlock's Last Case*—claimed Doc Watson got so fed up with Mr. Sherlock that he tried to murrrderrr his 221 Baker Street roommate."

Yeah, Max agreed there oughta be a law against two-bit scribblers of fake case reports getting rich and famous for knock-off pastries. He himself, as an unsavvy teenaged kid, had been played for a chump by what he doped out years later as not just a carelessly misprinted *MAD Magazine* series about "Shermlock Shomes".

Fool him once, shame on fake news. Fool him twice, shame on…

Hmmm.

His also overweight pear-shaped protege would take up a lot of space inside a locked room, but if confronted by a wrong-handed Sherlockian "orchestration" during tonight's Fun-'n'-Game charity event…

Hmmm.

Max decided to have the kid listen-and-learn as Yours Truly's "date" at a just-for-fun game afoot in *Case of an Escape Room Escapade*.

CHAPTER TWO

Flanked on the right by Police Chief Potter and on the left by a retired National Guard Major, "Stormin' Norman" McGrew—both in uniform, including headwear—Mayor Buford Bailey sat in the lap, so to speak, of the old "Gray Lady": a term for the town's most beloved architectural relic. At tables on the floor of the grand two-story banking hall—the Gray Lady's "torso", so to speak—leading citizens were seating themselves for a themed "Fun-'n'-Game" evening of dining, dancing, and, hopefully, fund raising.

Back in the day, the First National Bank of Henryetta had occupied the landmark structure known then by almost everyone in town as the "fat" Gray Lady within whose bowels most local wealth was lodged and…Buford himself now fondly recalled first coming into "her" presence as a lad with a paper route paycheck in hand…looking up with awe at the towering marble columns salvaged, people said, from ancient overseas ruins…looking left and right with awe at the polished round steel doors of the bank's dueling vaults at opposing ends of the torso… approaching the row of marble teller counters…and handing over his hard-earned wages for interest-bearing "digestion", so to speak.

A newspaper had later described the old Gray Lady as stubborn as a mule, "uglier and more "constipated" than someone named Victoria. But to Buford she was a queen who, unfortunately, aged through the years, not very gracefully. Most recently in the care of a so-called Pioneer State Bank, whose officials had restored the marble columns and other historic architectural features of the banking hall, only to declare she was bankrupt shortly afterward.

Abandoned and neglected for the past five years, tonight would be the once fat old lady's swan song, so to speak: a re-enactment, in a way, of her last gasps. Tomorrow, "she" would be bulldozed, her remains hauled off in pieces to the town dump to make room for his pet civic project, a parking lot.

Regretting that he had donned semi-formal civilian plaid for the occasion instead of his decorated red Shriner's uniform and tasseled fez cap, Buford stood, and...

"Welcome ladies and germs," he said into a handheld mic... which failed to get a single "ha" from the audience.

"The Open Sesame Foundation is dedicated to carrying out the federal government program to expose our children to hidden wonders of Arabian culture..."

Booo...

"...and last year raised over $2,000 for design and installation of a first piece of imaginatively themed playground equipment—called 'Jonah and The Whale'—for the new, ahem, Buford P. Bailey Park."

Booooo...

"This year, the foundation is in dire need of additional funds for, uh, refinement of the playground equipment and, uh, for settlement of certain related issues."

Booooooo...

"In support of the worthy cause, an anonymous donor has generously proposed this Fun-'n'-Game gala evening of dinner and dancing, as well as an entertaining 'escape room' challenge to honor the memory of the old Gray Lady."

Clap. Clap. Clap...

"A randomly selected group of citizens will seek refuge in the bank's safe-deposit-boxes vault and attempt to aid-and-abet tonight's, heh, heh, 'armed robbery', heh, heh. If the, heh, heh, 'thieves' escape the old lady's innards through the vault door locked tighter than a nun's, uh, purse from the outside, the anonymous donor has pledged a double-matching gift of up to $5,000 to the Open Sesame Foundation!"

Clap. Clap. Clap...

"To move things along, it is now my pleasure to introduce the team of game players," Buford bellowed to the now warmed-up assembly of potential co-donors.

"From London, England, but now living in Tulsa, Mr. Leroy Higgs, architectural designer responsible for the old Gray Lady's physical restoration to almost middle-aged beauty six years ago. Let's give Leroy the clap he deserves."

Clap. Clap. Clap…

"To provide additional inside know-how for an escape from the vault, also here with us is George McDonald, Pioneer Bank VP at the time of the Gray Lady's physical restoration, and later decline of her, uh, 'digestive' reliability, heh, heh. Now Vice-President of our still alive-and-kicking Farmers Credit Union… Welcome back to the 'innards', George."

Clap. Clap. Clap…

"At the anonymous donor's suggestion, not mine, Max Morgan…"

Clap.

"…along with a young lookalike, uh, assistant."

Clap. Clap.

"…will also take part.

Clap.

"More fittingly, in touching remembrance of both the old Gray Lady's demise — not to mention the unfortunate, uh, expiration of her late husband in the bowels of her — the Gray Lady's — aged body, we are honored that Mrs. Gladys Black has graciously returned to the scene of, uh, 'the crime', heh, heh. Let's have an especially warm welcome for the beloved widow of William 'Wild Bill' Black, who bravely gasped his last breath inside the safe-deposit-boxes vault."

Clap. Clap. Clap…

To a different audience Buford might have referred to Black's demise as having occurred *en flagrante*, as a bawdy Frenchman would say. Put delicately, Wild Bill's mismanagement and abuse had amounted to nothing less than ravishment of the old Gray Lady that had ensnarled depositors — Mayor to paperboys — in reams of federal red tape.

"And finally, to lead the team's mission to escape from the old Gray Lady's most private, uh, nook, seated beside me at the head table and ready to take charge is retired National Guard officer, Major Norman McGrew, who bravely served in Afghanistan…"

Clap. Clap. Clap. Clap. Clap. Clap. Clap…

"…and as a brave bank security guard…"

Clap. Clap.

… currently serving bravely as the local Walmart's Customer Complaint Manager."

Booooo….

"As we dine prior to waltzing to the music of the Bushwhacker Boys Orchestra, the team must escape the locked vault within an hour to qualify for the anonymous donor's generous pledge to the foundation. So without further ado, let's lock 'em up!"

Rah! Rah! Rah!…

As the orchestra began to tune up and other players retreated toward the vault behind the head table, Major McGrew stood, made a right-face maneuver and saluted. Buford picked up a manilla envelope from the table.

Rah! Rah! Rah!…

"Your orders, Major," he said, delivering the envelope to the mission leader, who took off his helmet, leaned closer, and—with steely-eyed resolve—listened intently as Buford launched into a meticulously detailed explanation of clues for escaping the old Gray Lady's rear vault.

Too much was at stake for an unorchestrated fun-and-game.

Rah! Rah! Rah!…

CHAPTER THREE

♫See that girl, barefootin' along/ Whistlin' and singin', she's carryin' on/ There's laughing in her eyes and dancing in her feet... ♫

Rah! Rah! Rah!...

With Bushwhacker Boys warming up and partygoers cheering, Max followed the Widow Black toward one of the two large, round steel doors at opposite ends of the old so-called banking hall.

♫So take off your shoes, and take off your hat/ Try on your wings and find out where it's at... ♫

Rah! Rah! Rah!...

The big steel door swung open. The widow shrank back. In a dreadful shuffling gait, Max edged past her and... after taking a deep breath...stepped through the round doorway into the old bank building's abandoned innard: a square room lined on three sides with numbered steel drawers of various sizes...steel table in the center, bolted to a polished concrete floor...steel ceiling with steel-encased light bulbs. In other words, closetrophobic in spades and impossible to escape...

Hmmm.

...unless the fund raising party game was a bait-and-switch joke, set-up to see if any player was quick enough on his feet to get out while the getting was good.

Bingo.

He turned to beat feet on the joke's punchline by "escaping" before the vault's thick steel door got shut behind him. But blocking his way out...

In came other game players: the kid, with a Sherlock Holmsian double-billed cap on his bean and unlit pipe clenched in his ivories...followed by the architect from Tulsa, Higgs, wearing a monogrammed all-black leisure suit and one of those floppy French beanies...followed by the former Pioneer Bank VP, McDonald, dressed in a businesslike three-piece pinstriped suit that—except for vest and only a single row of jacket buttons—almost matched the double-breasted duds worn by Yours Truly...followed by...

What in Sam Hill? The Widow Black—looking like a homeless bag lady draped in an old flour-sack of a dress and carrying a canvas tote with a faded Walmart logo on it—got down on her knees...put a bouquet of flowers on the concrete floor...crossed herself while silently moving her lips...and looked up with a prayerful expression in her watery eyes. Oh yeah, her Mister kicked a bucket on the premises five years ago; in suspicious and scandalous circumstances, he vaguely recalled.

With the vault door safely still open and the sixth game player, Major McGrew, not yet on the scene, Max doffed his fedora and paused to talk the talk before walking the walk:

"What we have here is an orchestrated situation set up to produce a half-baked pastiche of a classic locked-room murrrderrr mystery, in which..."

"Murrrderrr?" the Widow Black wailed, getting to her feet.

"...there would be no need for Yours Truly to dope out how someone would bump off a victim inside a locked room, or why," he explained. "The baked half-a-loaf would be how someone could get out of this 'oven' after the door got locked on the other side."

Ohhh, the others—except for the bookish kid—ohhhed.

"In the first murrrderrr mystery ever reported in pulp—*Case of Murder in the Rue Morgue*—an amateur French dick doped out that the doer of two broads found bosoms-up in a fourth floor room locked from inside, with no humanly way to safely escape through windows, was a runaway pet orangutang!"

Ohhh...

"And more than a hundred years later in *Case of the Speckled Band*," said the mouthy kid, increasingly inclined more to gabbing than jotting, "Mr. Sherlock Holmes deduced that a poisonous snake had been trained to enter and escape through an air vent."

"Snake!" the widow exclaimed.

"In Mr. Max's own recent *Case of Locked in the Loo...*"

"No need to get into that pastiche," said Max. "In the more applicable and more reliably reported *Case of the Married Virgin*, the doer did the dastardly deed by pumping poison gas through air vents into a locked bedroom before the new bride became a married ex-virgin."

"Both snake and gas scenarios would be impossible in this, uh, case," said Higgs, the architect for the bank building's restoration six years ago. "The vault has no ducts or vents."

"Yeah, no ducts, no vents!" said McDonald, with an angry glare at Higgs. "No air! Damnit, you're to blame for...for what almost happened!"

Hmmm.

"She was unmarried at the time, but no virgin!" Widow Black shrieked. "Not by a long shot!"

Hmmm.

"Ducts and vents in the structure's extra-thick walls would have been impractical, and not in keeping with the building's historical landmark status," said the English-speaking architect. "And besides, McDonald, you and your boss, the late unlamented William 'Wild Bill' Black, cut corners at every step of the restoration, supposedly to 'save the bank's money', but I suspect..."

"How dare you cast aspersions on my late husband's reputation!" the widow weakly protested. "Bill Black — may he rest in peace — was uh, a thrifty man."

"Not all locked-room mysteries involve murrrderrr, or even actual death," said the kid, putting a comforting arm around the now weeping Widow Black's scrawny shoulders. "In Mr. Percy Wilson's famous *Case of RSVP for a Funeral*, for instance — somewhat like *The Mystery of Edwin Drood* case report jotted by Mr. Charles Dickens—the 'victim' simply disappeared in circumstances that suggested murrrderrr. His plan was to put a cat among pigeons, so to speak, see how survivors reacted, and dope out who wanted him dead."

"Yeah, and Wild Bill Black was not the most likable guy in town," said McDonald, the ex-bank president's former assistant.

"But he didn't 'just disappear'!" the still grieving widow protested. "Not by a long shot!"

"And even in cases involving death, murrrderrr is not always afoot," the overly talkative kid needlessly pointed out. "In *Case of the Yellow Room* it turned out that a man inside a locked room had simply fell out of bed, bumped his head and…"

"Yeah, a simple case of accidental bucket-kicking," Max added, to reclaim the talking-points podium. "And in Percy Wilson's *Case of Stroke of Bad Luck* a joker inside a locked room had an unlucky brain stroke, also stumbled around in a confused condition, knocking over furniture that sounded like evidence of a struggle to others in the house, and also went toes-up due to natural cause."

Ohhh…

"Or the dead man could have been poisoned like the victim in *Case of Worse Late Than Never,*" Max continued talking the talk. "Survived long enough to go into a room, lock the door behind him, noisily stumble around and also kick a bucket."

Ohhh…

"My Bill was struck with a heart attack, but the vault's door was shut tighter than a mule's asshole, and no one heard him cry out for a doctor."

Yeah, too bad Yours Truly was not on the scene. In *Father Brown's Case of Thieves in Paradise* a corpse was found inside a locked bank vault. Ha! Oldest trick in the book: the doer had wedged an ice cube into the door's locking mechanism that—when the cube melted—allowed the mechanism to lock the door tighter than a wet boot a half-hour after he skated.

"Or a victim could be drugged, like in *The Verdict Case* from back in the *Noir,*" the kid again needlessly noted. "In that locked-room so-called mystery the worried group that knocked down the door the next morning included the would-be killer, who then offed the victim with a knife when the others, in panic, ran for a doctor."

"Bill was not deceased when they finally got the vault door open," the Black widow wailed. "I rolled him over to…to apply artificial exspiration. But it took that old doc an hour to get here. By then it was already too late—and unnecessary—for anyone to murder Bill."

Hmmm.

Max had a hunch he may have stumbled onto the scene of a crime dating back to when the bank was still in business. But before he could walk the walk…

"Drop your socks and grab your jocks!'

…striding through the still open vault doorway came the retired National Guard Major, currently an especially unhelpful clerk at Walmart who…

Oh no…

Clank!

Max hotfooted toward the vault's now closed thick steel door, but…

Clink!

…found himself stuck in a locked-room mystery, possibly in tight quarters with the doer of an unsolved murrrderrr!

CHAPTER FOUR

Leroy Higgs stood at rigid attention, holding a palm-forward British Army salute above his right eye. As a lad growing up in England, he had wanted to be a soldier—not to fight, only to wear a to-die-for uniform—but his parents had disapproved of a military career after seeing the Queen's Coldstream Guards march in a parade, attired in "dressy" kilts.

At ease, soldiers!" Major McGrew barked.

Leroy dropped his hand and...

"Smoke 'em if you got 'em."

...reflexively reached for a pocket before remembering that his stunning *Yves Saint Laurent* outfit had no pockets, and that he smoked only an occasional cigar inside a closet at home. His parents had also disapproved of tobacco usage, cigars in particular, after seeing the impeachment trial of President Clinton on the telly.

"I am this brokedick unit's CO, Major McGrew, RET," the major shouted. "Plain 'Sapper' to the few VFWs who also survived Explosive Ordnance Disposal duty in the Afghan sandbox. To you dogfaces, I am 'Sir' or 'Major' to my face. Behind my back: the 'Old Man' or 'Old Ironsides' or 'Old Shock-and-Awe'. Do you hear me?!"

"Affirmatory, Sir Major!" only Leroy answered.

"Jackson is hereby appointed to serve as my X-NCO for C-3," the CO hollered, with an errant point of a swagger stick. "Any FAQs, go through Jackson. But no, I repeat, no Mother McCreas! Any sob stories on your puny chests, take 'em to the chaplain. Do you hear me?!"

"Affirmatory, Sir Major, but it's 'Higgs', by the way. And if I may suggest, due to poor acoustics inside this confined steel space, there's no need for you to shout so loud."

"Damn right I'm proud! Thanks to National Guard DETON of enemy IEDs and friendly EOD FUBARS in Ghan, jarheads are not the only proud, and damn sure not the only few. Nine out of ten sappers of BRAVO CO, 45th INF BRIG made angel flights home in ten to twenty body bags. Do you grunts hear me?!"

"Affirmatory again, Sir Major, but if I may, YRU shouting in SMS language?"

The CO gave him one of those blank thousand-yard stares said to be typical of combat veterans, while fidgeting with what appeared to be strings dangling from inside his helmet.

"Mr. Higgs a/k/a 'Jackson' means why are you speaking in Short Message Language a/k/a text," the overweight teenaged team member yelled at the CO.

"Yeah, WTF?" McDonald yelled.

"Do I have to spell it out for you sadsacks? Yours not to wonder Whiskey-Hotel-Yankee. Under orders loud-and-clear from C-in-C Bailey, what's Nectar-Echo-X-Ray-Tango is for you G.I. Josephs to recon the right holes for these EOD fuses," said the major, opening a manilla envelope and dumping onto the vault's steel table...

"There are one, two, three... six of 'em, so at least one or two of you sappers has a Five Zero-Five One or Two chance to bug out of Hotel Haji alive, maybe even in one or two pieces."

"Begging your pardon, Sir Major," said Leroy, after moving closer to the steel table where six rings of paired bank-and-customer safe deposit box keys were strewn. "These, uh, possibly 'keys' to figuring out how to escape from this vault appear to not be 'fuses', but perhaps 'clueses'. We are, after all, playing only a game for charity."

"Perfect clarity," said the CO, before retrieving and putting under his helmet what might have been hearing aids previously dangling on wires. "Now, who's to be voluntold to set off the first

Explosive Ordnance Detonator?"

Leroy made an about-face maneuver, but…

"You, Jackson," the Old Man only semi-roared, not at him but at the overweight teenaged team member, "you look to be junior in rank and an old school doughboy sized to buffer an EOD blast. "Take these matched fuses numbered, uh, 6167431, locate the matching booby-trapped steel box and put fire in the hole. But—I repeat, but—hangfire until I give the order. Do you hear me?!"

"Hold your water, Major," said the also overweight middle-aged team member dressed in an unfashionably outdated double-breasted suit, floral tie and fedora. "Max Morgan's the name, private dicking's my game, and the kid is a protege of sorts: drafted into this outfit by Yours Truly. So fair's fair. Let McDonald here do the fire-in-the-hole honors. He was the VIP VP when the Pioneer Bank went tits-up, and is known to have inside know-how."

"Not me," said McDonald, the also middle-aged former bank Vice-President, who had abetted the former President, William Black, in undermining the historic building's restoration—and, no doubt, the bank's finances—by 'skimming' funds from the restoration budget. For the contents of one of the vault's steel boxes to blow up in the skimmer's face would serve him right, but…

"I'm still a VIP VP, at the Farmers Credit Union," McDonald whined, "bound by oath to not even peek inside a customer's safe deposit box, and too VIP to be put in danger."

Hopefully, the major would now assign to Black's widow the task of putting the numbered "fuses" into the keyhole of the matching-numbered safe deposit box. Though not exactly a thief, Mrs. Black's "decoration" of the grand banking hall—painting the magnificent Corinthian columns pink among other tasteless touches—had required expensive sandblasting that ate into the restoration budget. As a result—to add insult to injury, as it were—her now late husband had cancelled a Princess Diana-with-Fawn sculptural tableau that would have earned him—the project designer—a spread in *Architectural Digest*. But…

Oh no, to possibly add injury to insult…

"Looks like you've been voluntold to put fire in the first holes, Jackson," said Old Ironsides, extending a hand holding the selected ring of safe deposit keys… Phew!…not to him but to the overweight and unfashionably attired private detective.

"No way, José," said the fat man, backing away with hands held up. "Yours Truly is bound by a P.I. oath that in this case… Someone has to be voluntold to stand in the rear, to buffer the backside of the Widow Black in case coins and sharp pieces of jewelry ricochet off the steel ceiling when that suspicious box blows open."

"Courts martial and Section 8 discharges for you two gutless goldbricks," said the Sir Major, striding toward box number 6167431 with the keys in hand. "YOLO!"

Leroy fell to the floor. Both McDonald and Mrs. Black toppled on top of him… followed by—to judge by the impact—the overweight private detective, but…

He heard no BOOM, only the repetitive tinkling of what sounded like a wound-up music box. Out of the pile and onto his feet…

"I only know two tunes," said Old Shock-and-Awe, now with his helmetless, buzz-cut prematurely gray head leaned over the safe deposit box lying open on the steel table. "One an old barrack room ballad, the other one not. And…by gunnery, this is the very song my grandfather and other WWII vets used to sing at annual VFW BBQs."

Inside the opened box a statuette of a monkey working for an old-fashioned organ grinder held out a cup…and by golly, the middle-aged Old Man broke into song:

♫This is number one/ and the fun has just begun/ Roll me over, lay me down, and do it again/ Do it again, do it again/ Roll me o-o-over in the clo-o-over/ Roll me over, lay me down, and do it again…♫

"Those lyrics must be a clue for how to escape from the bank vault," said the teenager, who must have remained standing when the CO "put fire in the holes".

Cheese-and-crackers! He had missed a chance to be a hero that his parents would approve of, Leroy realized, with a frustrated stomp of a stylishly-shod foot! But... ♫Roll me over♫ he sang. ♫Roll me over, lay me down, and do it again... ♫

CHAPTER FIVE

♫This is number two/ and my hand is on her shoe/ Roll me over, lay me down, and do it again…♫

Max watched and listened as Major McGrew sang a second verse to the tune tinkled by a second monkey popped out of a second safety deposit box …

♫**Roll me o-o-over in the clo-o-over/ Roll me over, lay me down, and do it again…**♫

…and as other escape team members now sang along…

♫**Roll me o-o-ver in the clo-o-ov-er…**♫

Yours Truly saved his breathe and—looking at his watch—worried there would not be enough oxygen inside the airtight vault for the escape game to go on for the rest of the hour Mayor Bailey had announced as a time limit.

"My turn," said the Anglo apple polisher, Higgs, bounding toward another numbered steel box with a ring of numbered keys in hand.

"Open, Sesame!"

♫This is number three/ and my hand is on her knee…♫ the Major sang to the same tune.

♫**Roll me o-o-over in the clo-o-over/ Roll me over, lay me down, and do it again…**♫

Fine, let the over-the-hill National Guard songbird and chorus line spin wheels in the fun-and-game—or rather no fun-and-no game—based on the kid's WAG a/k/a wild-ass-guess that something contained in one or more of the safety deposit boxes would somehow lead to escape from the bank vault. Yours Truly would keep his powder dry and…

"Jackson! You're Nectar-Echo-Xray-Tango in this Ruskie Roulette OP," the so-called CO barked, aiming his stick at McDonald, the ex-bank VP. "You've got at best Two-to-One odds that box number 6953704 doesn't have your name on it. Suck it up, soldier!"

Max's brain—that he sometimes thought of as a hamster inside his head—continued to spin its own wheel.

♫This is number four/ and her husband's at the door/ Roll me over, lay me down, and do it again... ♫

♫Roll me o-o-over, in the clo-o-over/ Roll me over, lay me down, and do it again... ♫

Yeah, the real locked-room game afoot in *Case of Escape Room Escapade* was doping out what person or persons unknown might have had a murrderrrous hand in the death five years ago of the ex-bank President, William "Wild Bill" Black.

♫This is number five/ and I'm lucky to be alive... ♫

♫Roll me over in the clover, and do it again... ♫

The Widow Black had admitted to rolling over her husband after finding him unconscious on the floor inside the vault, and claimed she had tried to revive her spouse by so-called artificial "expiration". Yeah, maybe by intentionally sucking instead of blowing.

♫Roll me o-o-over... ♫

"Who's Nectar-Echo-Xray-Tango?!" McGrew shouted. "Uncle Sam expects every nephew to do his duty."

On the other hand, Higgs, the architect who'd been in charge of the bank building restoration a year before Black's death on the premises, had as much as accused the ex-Prexy of grafting funds budgeted for the project.

On the other other hand, McDonald had outrightly and heatedly accused Higgs of being responsible for the vault having no air vents, and for "what almost happened".

On a third hand, so to speak, the Mayor had said both the project architect <u>and</u> ex-bank VP had knowledge about the old Gray Lady's "innards", but...

Hmmm.

Though now seeming to have had a falling out, the two insiders may have been in cahoots with one another.

Hmmm.

The Widow Black staggered forward, clutching a sixth key in a trembling hand, but…

"WACLICO!" the major shouted, with a shake of his head and thrust of his jaw that caused what looked to be strings to again drop from inside his helmet. "For you untrained thirty-day wonders, that means WOMEN AND CHILDREN LAST IN COMBAT OPS! Especially for suicide missions."

Ohhhhh, the "nephews"—except Yours Truly—ohhhhhed.

"Don't ask and I won't tell!" McGrew then only semi-shouted after getting in the face of Higgs. "Sorry, Jackson, that facial hair drooping from your upper lip disqualifies you for Section 8 Discharge during a DEFCON DETON OP. Into the sixth holes, soldier, on the double!"

"Wait a minute, Sir Shock-and-Awe," said the British suck-up. "The last numbers on the boxes and matching, uh, 'fuses' that we've tried so far are in a sequence of 1-2-3-4-5. So…"

"This key number ends with a 6!" the widow shrieked."

"No sick call, I repeat, no sick call for Forward Operating Base personnel during a DEFCON DETON OP!"

"Gimme that!" said McDonald, snatching the key from the Black broad's still outstretched hand, then and shouting at the major: "Damnit, put your hearing aids back in your ears and listen!"

Ohhhhh…

"Do your duty, Jackson! Missin' a few body parts is better than full-body MIA. Man up and put fire in the sixth holes. TNT!"

Ohhhhh…

"That's TODAY NOT TOMORROW, soldier!"

Ohhhhh…

"I only got a glance before Black tucked it away, but a secret combination for emergency unlocking of the…"

Ohhhhh…

"Secret combination for emergency escape?!" Higgs exclaimed.

"Why?...Why?...Why, for God's sake, a secret combination? And why the hell didn't you speak up sooner?!"

"TNT! soldier. That's an order!"

Eyeing a circular gadget that looked to be a useless thermostat control monitor mounted to the wall next to the vault door, the ex-bank VP—in a sweat—explained that he had just then recalled that a secret numerical combination for unlocking the vault might have ended with a 6.

Ohhhhh...

"Again, you idiot, a 'secret combination' for emergency escape?!" Higgs again shouted. "Why?...Why?...For God's sake, why?" the het-up Brit sputtered.

Provision for emergency escape from locked vaults was required by bank regulators, McDonald further explained. Standard arrangements included a device for triggering ventilation, a phone for sounding an alarm, a key or coded combination for unlocking a vault door, and instructions that—at the old Pioneer State Bank—were kept inside a safe deposit box inside the vault. But audits of such arrangements were rare and...

"What would be the point of having instructions locked in an unidentified safe deposit box, you idiot?" said Higgs, throwing his black cap onto the floor.

"Old man Black was a corner-cutter, trusted no one and was secretive by nature," said the deceased ex-bank President's ex-assistant, loosening his tie.

"But presumably not completely stupid," said Higgs. "My God, what if the steel door had been accidentally closed and locked while a safe deposit customer was inside?"

"Black didn't give a shit about customers. He didn't trust and didn't give a shit about anyone but himself."

"I refuse to stand by and have memory of my late husband defiled by the likes of you, George McDonald, a blind fool and a little too 'trustworthy' about certain personal matters!"

"Damnit, McDonald, it's your fault Major Shock-and-Awe has had to put us through this...this shock and awe?"

"I don't give a shit about a donation for 'refinement' of that playground piece of junk you designed. It ought to be scrapped before…"

As the architect and banker started throwing knuckle sandwiches at each other, Max stepped back a peg.

"Order in the ranks!" McGrew roared. "Hand over those fuses, Jackson!" he then barked at McDonald. "As CO in this brokedick unit, I myself will put fire in the holes of the last no doubt booby-trapped box."

"No need to put your brass in harm's way yet, Major," said the kid. "At least not until dialing a simple sequence ending with a 6 into that emergency unlocking device."

"Yes!" the Widow Black screeched. "Dial a 1-2-3-4-5-6 combination and let me out of here, you little pimp!"

Hmmm.

As McDonald began to dial the wall-mounted gizmo right-and-left, Max held his breath.

"Open Sesame!" Higgs hollered, but…

"No dice," said the ex-bank VP, turning from the dial to face the other escape team members. "1-through-6 is not the combination for emergency escape."

Ohhhhh…

Max again looked at his watch. More than thirty minutes had passed since the vault door got slammed shut.

No doubt the Mayor would also be nervously keeping time at the banking hall's head table — not realizing that Yours Truly was trapped inside the steel box with possibly a murrrderrrer — but beginning to worry that the escape team had not yet — and might not ever — qualify for a $5,000 anonymous donation to the Open Sesame Foundation.

CHAPTER SIX

What the heck:

Though almost finished dining and ordinarily only a ceremonial sipper, Buford — still seated at the gala charity event's head table — waved for a waiter to pour another glass of wine.

The Open Sesame Foundation had emptied its coffers to put on the Fun-'n'-Game event, and the "fun" part was working like a charm. Potential donors swilling imported vino at tables inside the old Gay Lady's former banking hall had to be already in a mood to belly-up at least $2,500 to qualify for the anonymous benefactors double-matching gift of $5,000, and dancing had not yet begun.

Funds in those amounts, if not more, were desperately needed to settle...

"Why did you happen to put that odd-ball architect from Tulsa on the vault escape team?" said Police Chief Potter, as though reading his mind from beside him at the head table. "He's the guy who botched the foundation's sponsorship of that playground equipment. Heck, that little girl was almost a teenager by the time we got her out."

"She was well fed, comfortable and completely safe during her, uh, confinement," said Buford as the waiter filled his glass. "Dog-gone-it, Chief, you should have consulted higher authority, namely me, before resorting to extreme measures. Now everyone, including the girl's parents and their lawyer, are calling the 'Jonah and the Whale' attraction 'Jaws of Death'."

"Dang it, Buford, she was trapped inside that steel fish for days before I called in the 'Jaws of Life' equipment, and you were nowhere to be found. That foreign architect claimed you yourself…"

"Open-and-shut case of parental neglect according to my, I mean the town's legal mouthpiece. To semi-quote President Lyndon Johnson—one of my political role models—better to keep Higgs inside the tent, urinating outward. Honoring, or at least, uh, recognizing the playground equipment designer will remind the public that he did good work on the old Gray Lady a few years back."

"Yeah, but the whole idea of a steel sea monster with open-and-shut, uh, mouth…The wife and her Bible study group say 'Jonah and the Whale' is a Hebrew story, not really eligible for the federal grant you got for opening kids' eyes to Arab culture."

"The town's only resident of Arab persuasion, Mohammed Johnson, assures me that his bible includes the same story and same moral to obey authority figures such as God, and elected officials," Buford explained. "The big blue whale attraction on Route 66 in Catoosa has drawn millions of tourists through the years without unfortunate incidents of, uh, parental neglect."

"Okay, you're the Mayor and honorary foundation chairman," Potter recognized, before draining his own glass, waving, and then…

"Why George McDonald?" asked the uppity policeman of lower civic rank. "Bringing the ex-Pioneer Bank VP into the 'tent' is likely reminding people of already unforgotten scandal."

Scandal?

Buford—bristling at the suggestion of fellow Shriner involvement in misbehavior—again waved.

Yes, the armed robbery five years ago had brought to light Wild Bill Black's mismanagement and might have hastened the Pioneer Bank going rupt, but…

"State and federal investigators were suspicious about so much cash supposedly being out of the vault and in the banking hall teller drawers: ninety thousand, as I recall," the Chief nevertheless gossiped. "But since Black had died of a heart attack during the robbery, other details were…Well, my Missus and her

Canasta group still cluck."

Canasta clubs!

As a dedicated public servant, Buford himself had sometimes been the target of clucking by female idlers, often actually and... Yes, admittedly, George McDonald had gone through a period of occasional, uh, over-tippling in the aftermath of the bank robbery. But heck, his fiancee, Janie Feinstein—cute as a button and smart as an acre of garlic—had almost expired during the upsetting incident. Now George was married to Janie and always sober as a judge. Yet clucking card players...

"As a matter of fact, I had to talk McDonald into being part of the escape team," Buford explained, after gulping down his glass of wine and waving for more. "Both a qualified marriage counselor and AA sponsor advised that he, uh, re-live in a way and put behind them the trauma of what he—and Janie—went through."

"Okay," said the Chief. "I'm not one to spread official police information, but... Mayor, why in blazes did you put that retired National Guard nutcase and Max Morgan on the escape team? McGrew is, literally, a loose cannon. Morgan, as a so-called 'private investigator'—through not just a so-called 'Fat Man'—couldn't detect his own rear end if he searched with both hands, and that's sayin' somethin'."

Feeling grilled by the town's top cop, Buford—deeming a pending personal complaint about a faulty Walmart home appliance not relevant—dodged vouching for McGrew, and explained only that the charity event's anonymous would-be donor had insisted that Morgan actually lead the escape team—possibly because of a prior engagement of the so-called gumshoe's services—but that on his own initiative...

"All the more puzzling," the Chief countered. And in fact Max Morgan was known for his unerring ability to make hash out of simple-as-pie, uh, "engagements".

Feeling compelled to further explain—and further assure himself that "hash" would not be served for dessert at the head table, so to speak—Buford leaned toward the Chief's ear and in a lowered voice confided that he had personally recruited Major McGrew to take charge of the vault escape game, and hinted that an, uh, "orchestrated" outcome of the game was in the works.

"That could be viewed as fraudulent tampering, Buford. As the town's Chief of Police, my duty…"

"I simply handed over the simple clues to the major and carefully went over detailed instructions key-by-key three times," Buford confided. "To have put Gladys Black at risk of running out of air inside that steel, uh, enclosure would have been, uh, criminal."

Satisfied by the local chief law enforcement officer's silent nod that he was not at risk of being arrested for his harmless "orchestration" of only a game—staged for a worthy cause—Buford tipped back his chair and glass, then waved for another ceremonial drop of vino in celebration of his good works for the Open Sesame Foundation.

CHAPTER SEVEN

Max took off his felt fedora, loosened his floral tie, undid the top button of his sweat-soaked shirt, and again checked his watch. Only when released from the overheated vault would Yours Truly be able to safely open a cold-case investigation into the suspicious death of William "Wild Bill" Black on the premises five years ago, but…

Air inside the vault had gotten stale as a two-day-old biscuit. Nerves of the other occupants were crumbling like the crusts of three-day-old biscuits. Tension was thick enough to spread on a…In other words, though he was peckish, the situation was "unappetizing", and getting more so. He was stuck in the "Old Gray Lady's colon", as the Mayor might have put it. Not even a germ could get through the old bank's puckered "anus", so to speak. Continued effort to escape would be a waste of gas remaining in his tank.

In other words, with fifteen minutes of "playing time" remaining, the name of the game had changed from escape to rescue.

McGrew had already set "fuses" in a sixth safe deposit container. To the tune of another music box, the wacko military veteran had sung ♫This is number six/ and I'm in an awful fix♫ But no soap. Now the hardheaded National Guard major was trying to insert keys into one after another of the old bank's dozens of other locked safe deposit boxes, hoping to find emergency escape instructions. Yeah, maybe along the lines of a musical "IED" tinkling the tune of, say, ♫This is number eight/ and the way to open the gate♫.

Also pointlessly, the kid was wasting the vault's waning supply of oxygen by continuing to spout details of inapplicable gumshoe case reports from back in the *Noir* and beyond. He'd already recited in detail the famous longwinded lecture listing the seven scenarios for locked-room mysteries delivered in *Case of the Hollow Man* by the famous amateur sleuth, Dr. Gideon Fell. Finally focused on case report set-ups for getting in and out of locked-rooms — as opposed to howdidit and whodunnit angles of murrrderrr methods and identification of doers — the young would-be P.I. had raised multiple impossible possibilities.

And now, with an index finger pointed upward as though a bright idea had popped into his bean...

"Lots of locked-room murrrderrr mysteries involve physical, even 'architectural' tampering of one kind or another," said the young case report jotter and protege. "In Mr. Percy Wilson's *Case of Pane in the Rear*, for instance, a handyman escaped from a locked back room by breaking a window, then replaced the glass from outside."

"Astute 'detection' by Mr. Wilson," said Higgs in a sarcastic tone of voice. "But as any fool can see, this vault has no panes, only a 'pain in the rear'. McDonald is handy at tampering with bank books alright, but..."

"No windows and no f'ing air vents!" McDonald shouted, with a returned angry glare at the architect. "But speaking of architectural tampering, why the hell did you insist on removal of the lever for emergency manual-opening of the vault door from inside the banking hall?"

"The lever was ugly," said the fancy-pants architect, "utterly out of sorts with stylish architectural aesthetics."

"For crying out loud, delay in getting the door open after the robbery almost resulted in..."

"Black himself ordered the lever's removal, maybe to keep Nosy Nellies from interrupting what he had an illicit habit of doing in here."

Higgs and McDonald squared off for another round of fisticuffs, each giving the other an Evil-Eye Fleagle double whammy powerful enough to make the Mount Rushmore head of Theodore Roosevelt weep.

The Widow Black—hunkered in a corner of the vault—directed at both Higgs and McDonald a Fleagle triple whammy that would have melted a battleship.

"What I was getting to is that one of these safe deposit 'drawers' might be a false front that conceals a hidden compartment," said the kid, moving toward the corner where the old widow woman sat on the floor, clutching her canvas tote. "In *Case of the Doctor's Case*, as a matter of fact, Dr. Watson solved a murrrderrr committed inside a supposedly empty locked room by detecting what even Mr. Max—I mean Mr. Sherlock—had failed to notice."

Max bit his lip as his soon-to-be ex-protege continued to spout.

"A photorealistic painting of a section of Turkish rug and lower portion of a bookcase—mounted between two coffee-table legs—made it appear that nothing but floor and air was under the table, masking a hidden compartment and creating a hidey-hole inside the locked room."

"Brilliant detective work, 'Watson'," McDonald snarled. "Higgs must have hid under the steel able, bumped off Black, got back under the table and—when the coast was clear—escaped from the vault by repeatedly yelling 'Open Sesame!' Like he did when..."

"The playground whale was not constructed to my specifications!" Higgs shouted at the ex-bank VP. "The Mayor is Honorary Chairman of the Open Sesame Foundation, and you are his fraternal bootlicker who no doubt abetted the skimping-and-skimming on the emergency escape mechanism, just like you and Black did on the system for emergency escape from this damned vault!"

"I was once a Shriner, yeah, but was never in cahoots with Black. I hated the son-of-a-bitch!"

Hmmm.

"Stand down, Jackson!" Major McGrew roared, pushing

the kid aside and barging into the corner. "Stand up, Ma'am!" the "sapper" then shouted at the Widow Black, who was now munching a sandwich she must have had stashed in her tote. "This corner box is big enough to hold a WMD that could blow at any second!"

"Mind your manners, Major!" the ladylike but understandably irritable old woman shouted at the major. "I'm having my supper."

"Yeah, enough already with you and your confusing 'fusing' bullshit," McDonald added.

"Another insubordinate peep from you, Jackson, and your ass is outa here! Do you hear me?!"

"I hear you loud and clear, Sir Shock-and-Awe!" Higgs bellowed, with another snappy salute and click of his heels. "'Jackson'—the ex-bank VP 'Jackson'—is to blame for every foul-up at this bank, from six years ago to now. He deserves to be stripped of his, uh, pinstripes!"

"The correct term is 'fubar', soldier, which—for the benefit of you Johnnys-Come-Marching-Latelies—means fouled-up beyond all recognition."

"Understood, Sir Major. *Hugo Boss* knock-offs are almost all fubars."

"Make them both pay!" Old Lady Black shrieked.

"Order in the ranks!" Major McGrew shouted.

Uh oh, the architect and ex-bank VP were rolling around on the concrete floor in an obviously unfriendly embrace.

Max checked his watch. Seven minutes remained in the rigged hourlong game. Yeah, the charity event's "entertainment" had been orchestrated alright, possibly to prompt an investigation by Yours Truly into the can of worms related to William Black's likely murrrderrr five years ago, but…Though rescue was sure to be near at hand, he crossed his fingers, worried that the whole vault would blow—not necessarily by DETON of an IED or WMD—but more likely by spontaneous combustion of overheated human gases!

CHAPTER EIGHT

Gladys Black sat on the floor in a corner of the vault... still clutching her canvas bag to her breast as a mother would cling to a child...back to holding in her hand a safe-deposit-box key as a Catholic martyr would cling to a crucifix...silently bemoaning the cruel injustice she endured.

At the age of sixty-five, there she was, miserably trapped inside the Pioneer Bank's long abandoned vault and gasping for air, not ten feet from where her bouquet of wilting flowers marked the spot where she had found her late husband drawing his last breath in a, uh, unseemly circumstances. Now she herself would expire in an off-key reprise of her prior abject humiliation. From his grave, William Black would have the last laugh.

Yes, in her naive youth she was a "princess" and had "set her cap" for Billy Black, as her disapproving old-fashioned mother would have, and in fact did say. Was that such a sin? Bill was not a "Prince Charming", not by a long shot, but young, marginally not unattractive back then, drove a shiny red sports car and was known to splurge. He was not older, previously married, and a boring doctor like her high school classmate, Candice Wallace, had bed-and-wed when she also approached the dreaded age of thirty.

And Bill Black was set to inherit majority ownership of the Pioneer Bank, where they both worked, and where she had imagined they would reign together as king and queen. Yes, the pregnancy alarm had proven to be false. Yes, her disapproving mother, immediately, and Bill later, had cruelly accused her of "entrapment". But...

"Gonna have to blow that corner box!" barked the military officer Mayor Bailey had unwisely assigned to the so-called escape team.

Gladys clutched her canvas bag tighter as she scooted from her spot on the floor.

Wild Bill Black was a "catch" alright, and got richer after becoming the bank's majority shareholder and CEO. But in his dealings with her — his wife and partner — he was a miserable miser. A character flaw all the more unforgivable, given that he secretly squandered their marital assets on...Well, she was not stupid. That little Miss Feinstein — dark, wiry, black eyes always darting here-and-there as she licked her always glossy red lips — was a snake!

As the CEO's spouse, however — though forced out of a salaried bank position-- she herself had continued to have run of the place, including Bill's private office. And there it was: stashed in a metal box — locked, but not securely enough — along with other secret documentary evidence of illegal dealings involving tens of thousands of dollars.

A tear fell as Gladys recalled finding a cancelled check made out to a Tulsa jewelry store in payment for — her justified "snooping" soon also uncovered — an expensive gold bracelet never seen by her up to then! But later...

"The safe deposit boxes are organized into two sections on each of three walls, Mr. Max," the overweight teenaged boy pointlessly announced, before also noting that the boxes were semi-sequentially numbered — with a few gaps — "from 6167431 to 6643892 to 6957583 to..."

"Forget the math," the fat so-called private detective advised. "The numerical so-called clues for blowing this pop stand add up to zilch."

"As you were, soldiers! This big corner-box has been monkeyed with, left partially open, but is stuck in its slot tighter than three grunts in a one-man foxhole."

"Hangfire, McGrew! A live, and large monkey could be inside that box. And rescue is at hand!"

Gladys sighed. Was spending her last minutes of life in the company of such nitwits her reward for being charitable? She herself had nominated the overweight so-called "gumshoe" to be part of the so-called escape game after hearing his mother—a Canasta club member—wail that the middle-aged son was a Notary Public and so-called private eye whose recent "dickwork" inside a locked bathroom had been embarrassingly bungled. Out of pity, she had prevailed upon Mayor Bailey to...

"Uh! Uh! Uh! the other nitwit grunted as he struggled to open the big box.

"Allow me lend a hand, Sir Major," Leroy Higgs gratuitously volunteered.

What a duplicitous derriere kisser! The so-called architectural designer had crudely eradicated her redecoration of the banking hall and replaced her tasteful touches of color with so-called historical restoration of the building's hopelessly dull gray columns and other outdated features. For his one good idea...

Gladys ground her teeth.

Damnit, she had swallowed her pride and volunteered to collaborate with Mr. Higgs on design of a sculptural centerpiece for the re-done banking hall. And by inspirational coincidence the director of a touring Shakespearian musical called *Lady M for Murder* that came through Tulsa had recently given her a post-performance backstage compliment of being "Queenly in an Elizabethan sort of way", but...

To her shock and dismay, the preliminary half-size plaster model that showed up, instead of even resembling the photograph of herself that she'd submitted... "Diana-with-Fawn"?! How absurd, and how cruelly telling. The indecent almost naked "inspiration" for the pre-production model had obviously been none other than the so-called fiancee of George McDonald, the floozie who later showed up in the flesh, wearing...

Gladys continued to grind.

To add insult to insult, now sitting on the floor across from her, Bill's scheming former assistant openly smirked, clearly confirming her long held suspicions. To advance his own ambitions, the oily ex-bank Vice President had pimped his so-called fiancee. Yes, George McDonald had had effectively murdered Bill by loosening the poisonous dark-haired snake into the "Garden of Eden".

Feeling faint, Gladys began to silently pray. Her return tonight to the "scene of the crime" had been to gloat, she mournfully confessed to herself. Alas, instead of having a last laugh, she would die a poor, lonely widow. For not getting what she deserved, contrary to what people would say, Bill would get the last laugh.

"Three!...Two!...One!"

"Open Sesame!"

Gladys held a possibly last breath...awaited a possibly last word...and heard...

"FUBAR!"

CHAPTER NINE

Woozier from lack of fresh air...desperate in the wake of McGrew's failure to find emergency escape instructions inside the safe deposit box he'd pried open...and with no rescue at hand... Max staggered to the vault's steel door, but...dang it, detected no puddle of water to indicate an ice cube possibly wedged into the locking mechanism might be melting.

He pressed an ear to the oddly cold steel, but...dang it, heard no clicking of tumblers to indicate a combination lock was being rolled on the other side.

The game was ten minutes into overtime, but...dang it, he heard no battering ram being pounded against the likely jammed door.

He swiveled and suspiciously eyed the motley crew of teammates.

The Pioneer Bank President, William Black, had kicked a bucket on the premises five years ago, and surviving spouses were usually suspects *Numero Uno*. Plus, killers were known to often return to the scenes of their crimes, but...

Max lost his train of thought.

Leroy Higgs — now standing at slightly slumped "attention" beside McGrew — was tight with the Mayor and the Open Sesame Foundation that together had promoted the Fun-'n'-Game set-up. Yeah, the foreign architect had something on his chest alright. A subtle but tell-tale YSL monogram on Higgs' black leisure suit was a sure tip-off that the foreign architect was a closet burglar and now operating under an alias. But...

In a near swoon, Max had a hazy hunch George McDonald

was the rigger of the game. Yeah, the ex-bank VP now cowering in a corner of the vault looked guilty, sickly, and — muttering to himself and sweating — maybe off his rocker. Maybe bent on suicidal revenge for…

"Remember the Alamo!" McGrew bellowed.

Max's ears perked up for a welcome pep talk.

"A small unit of brave Texicans were trapped at church, surrounded by hostile Mexican troops, running out of food, water and ammo."

"I can't say that I do recall an Alamo parish, Sir Major," Higgs responded. "But I've heard of Dunkirk Beach where a large number of brave British people were rescued by stylishly uniformed Coldstream Life Guards."

"Forget the Brit SNAFU, soldier! That's an order!"

Yessir!" said Higgs, with a lame hand salute and soft click of his heels.

"Remember Dien Bien Phu! Cowardly but allied Frogs were encirclement by Uncle Ho's Cong!"

"Yessir, I'll remember."

"Remember Bay of Pigs! Brave Cuban C.I.A. agents were stranded on a beachhead under fire from that Commie bastard, Fidel Castro!"

"Yessir, I'll try to…"

"Remember the Desert One FUBAR that left fifty-two scared-shitless American civilian hostages in the grip of that f'ing Ayo-yo-tollah!"

"Yessir, I'll…"

"Remember the FUBAR of Uncle Sam's brokedick retreat from the Ghan sandbox! Do you hear me?!"

Max heard, but was not pepped up.

"That's the straight unsugarcoated poop at 0:17 clicks past Zero Hour. Civilian chickenhawks have not left, I repeat, civilian desk jockeys have not left no one behind. Papa-Oscar-Golfs on the home front — that spells POGs, Persons Other than Grunts — have left everyone behind, again!"

"Oh," Max ohed.

"To spell it out for you trench monkeys, there will be no Romeo-Echo-Sierra-Quebec. I repeat, no R-E-S-Q from this FOB. So suck it up, soldiers. Write your Good Behavior letters to your old ladies, and prepare to make the ultimate sacrifice. No tears!"

"Damn Buford Bailey and that Police Chief!" McDonald wailed. "They're trying to break me, trying to pin me with guilt for what happened five years ago."

"You deserve to be pinned, you little prick!" Widow Black screeched, half-rising from the floor and shaking a bony fist at the former bank VP. "If you had kept that hot-to-trot so-called virgin fiancee of yours under lock-and-key of a chastity belt, my Bill would never have…had a heart attack!"

"Damn you <u>and</u> Black!" Higgs shouted, also shaking a fist at McDonald. "Our rescue is probably fouled up beyond all recognition like a cheap *Hugo Boss* knock-off because you two greedy bankers failed to keep this Old Gray Lady's locking mechanism well attended to and adequately lubricated!"

"You're a fine one to point fingers for faulty locking—and unlocking mechanisms—you little ponce. You hated Black for shit-canning that stupid design of a 'Diana-with Fawn' statue! And now our conniving Mayor is also pressuring you to take full responsibility for f'ing-up that 'unlubricated' whale in his park."

"Order in the ranks!" McGrew shouted.

"Yessir."

"Forget Mister Outside and remember Doc Blanchard!"

Max drew a blank.

"Blanchard a/k/a Mister Inside a/k/a the human battering ram led West Point's WWII undefeated Brave Old Army Team out of many a tight spot by bravely beating his head against steel walls put up to block his runs to daylight."

Old Shock-and-Awe tightened his helmet strap, jutted out his jaw, and leaned down with hands on his knees.

"You, Jackson, assume the position on my right flank," he ordered, with a nod at Higgs. "You, Jackson, bend over on my left flank," he commanded, with a steely glare at Yours Truly.

"We'll break out of this tight spot with a Flying Human Wedge!

"Hut! Hut! Hut! BOHICA!"

Max and Higgs remained rooted in place.

BANG!

"Revive Major Ironsides!" the kid hollered. "I think I've doped out the clues for how to get out of here alive!"

Max slumped to the floor, doubtful but hopeful that his teenaged protege had luckily stumbled onto a last-ditch play for Yours Truly to make a last-gasp run to daylight without risk of skull fracture.

CHAPTER TEN

♫I got a funny feelin'/ the moment your lips touched mine...♫

As one of the Bushwhacker Boys switched to singing words of a slow dance tune, Buford's toe stopped tapping. A tear almost ran down a cheek. He took another gulp of wine. The country-and-western song was like an echo of Wild Bill Black's wailing from inside the tomblike bank vault.

♫Somethin' shot right through me/ My heart skipped a beat in time...♫

Earlier, seeing Gladys Black limp into the vault with a bouquet of flowers in her arms had been slightly touching. Now the grieving widow's return to the scene of her husband's demise struck Buford—though a lifelong bachelor—as downright romanticly sentimental.

♫It got me to thinkin' crazy things/ I even think I saw a flash of light...♫

Admittedly, Bill Black, though a fellow Shriner, had been a hard man to like. And Gladys also had always been, uh, difficult to get along with. They had been known to fuss with one another. But what longtime married couple didn't often cuss each other like drunk sailors and throw pots and pans from time to time? At the end...

♫Girl, you've never moved me/ quite like you've moved me tonight...♫

"Gawkers who witnessed the touching scene of Wild Bill's passing say that Gladys rolled him over and gave him a last kiss," Buford said to Chief Potter, back to sitting beside him at the head table after a whirl on the dance floor.

♫You shouldn't kiss me like this...♫

"Yeah, some call mouth-to-mouth artificial respiration the 'Kiss of Life', but in the Blacks' case it was more like a blown-from-the-hand 'kiss-off'," said the unsentimental cop who had been one of the gawkers.

♫I think you mean it like that... ♫

"No way, Chief. I myself got to the bank just as they were rolling Bill out. Gladys' bright red lipstick was smeared all over his gray face."

"That wasn't Mrs. Black's lipstick, Buford."

"What? Blood? OMG, Bill must have taken a fall."

"Yeah, you could put it that way, but…I'm not one to tell tales but, you know, there was that young woman also in the vault when we got the door opened, also unconscious due to lack of oxygen."

Buford knew that. Janie McDonald *nee* Feinstein was a young underling at the bank at the time, a dark-haired beauty, slim and graceful as a cat. That's where she and George, uh, got together.

"Well, she was an 'underling' alright. Mrs. Black had to roll her husband off Miss Feinstein to blow that 'kiss' at his, uh, bright red face before going through his pockets and trying to take a gold bracelet off Miss Feinstein's wrist."

As Buford waved for another glass of wine, the Bushwhacker Boys appropriately changed their tune.

♫She was a woman on a mission/ Here to drown him and forget him... ♫

In vino *veritas*, as Italian Popes used to say. Truth be told, he'd always had a lowly opinion of Janie McDonald *nee* Feinstein. She was too good-looking and too frisky for George McDonald. And may have been the bad influence that drove the ex-bank VP to become too fond of vino. Though also a Shriner, George had not marched in parades following the bank failure, never again wore his fez in public, and was known to make uncomplimentary comments about his late boss and late fellow Shriner, Bill Black.

♫Why don't you kiss this/ And I don't mean my rosy red lips... ♫

Following a confidential chat with that AA do-gooder who

claimed to be a friend of Bill's, Buford, not one to judge — and he was up for re-election — had, uh, recognized George by getting him to be a Fun-'n'-Game participant.

As for the memory of Bill Black, he would not make excuses for Wild Bill's alleged, uh, wild behavior, but neither would he fault his fellow Shriner for, uh, making a bad choice. Men in uniform drew women like flies. A Shriner's tasseled fez, in particular, was like catnip to…to feline females.

And Bill had done right by Gladys when all was said and done, Buford assured himself before again gulping and waving.

♫**If you've got the money, honey, I've got the time…**♫

"You gotta feel bad for the cranky old gal," the Chief said. "On top of…I mean in addition to what Black put the wife through during their marriage, he seems to have left her penniless."

♫**Bring along your Cadillac, leave my old wreck behind…**♫

"I wouldn't worry about Gladys Black on that account, Chief. Wild Bill left his widow well fixed."

♫**We'll have lots of fun, honey, we'll be doin' fine…**♫

"Are you kidding? The poor old woman staggered into the vault wearing worn out high-top sneakers, a raggedy dress, and a bag lady's torn dirty tote fit for nothing but scavenging from garbage cans."

"We'll go honky-tonking, honey, we'll do it on your dime…♫

Though somewhat torn between keeping a sworn secret and standing up for a fellow Shriner…

"Just between you, me and the lamppost," Buford semi-whispered to his head table companion. "Gladys is a frugal, but…"

Feeling breach of a confidence was justified under the circumstances, Buford further stood up for a fellow Shriner's somewhat tattered reputation by confiding to Police Chief Potter that Bill Black's widow was the conditionally generous anonymous donor of $5,000 to the Open Sesame Foundation.

♫**If you've got no more money, honey, I've got no more time…**♫

CHAPTER ELEVEN

George needed a drink.

Contrary to the advice of his AA sponsor and that crackpot marriage counselor—not to mention the nagging insistence of his wife—the so-called escape-room "game" could not have been more devilishly designed for opening old wounds instead of healing his so-called "hang-ups".

Okay, William Black had once been a kindly-seeming "father figure" to him. Maybe by some kind of so-called "transference" of a so-called "Oedipus Complex" he had wanted to kill his deceitful mentor. But damnit, the old bastard got what he deserved. No way could there have been ninety-thousand bucks in teller cash drawers at the time of that so-called robbery. By hindsight, the tip-off that something off-key was being orchestrated was Black's hiring of …

"Just the usual ringing in the ears," the retired and now semi-revived National Guard officer was saying to Higgs. "Gonna have to blow the fronts off all these cans," the also former bank security guard insanely hollered. "Collateral casualties be damned!"

George—already nursing a blackened eye and bloody nose resulting from his scuffles with Higgs—shrank deeper into a corner.

"FUBAR! These surplus WWII EODs I carry for emergencies are as brokedick as this unit of dogfaces."

Another dud, thankfully, but talk about PSTD and needing to "take it to the chaplain": How many tons of guilty conscience for how many "collateral casualties"—both enemies and victims of "friendly fire"— did the military maniac have on his stuck-out chest?

For crying out loud, five years ago the moronic combat veteran hired by Black had hurled a grenade—thankfully another dud—at the so-called robbers escaping the banking hall. The seemingly insane act had not only been a distraction from what was going on, but left tellers and bank customers too traumatized to remember their own names, much less be of any assistance to investigators

And Higgs! There was a guy who should be committed to a psyco institution—if not jail—for well deserved guilt. Black had used him like a rented mule to, okay, probably to skim funds from the bank's architectural restoration budget, but hell, it was the costs of Leroy Higgs' grandiose designs that—as much as the "robbery"—had tipped the Pioneer Bank into insolvency. And that f'ing playground fish! How in hell would children know that yelling "Open Sesame" was an "entertaining" interactive audio trigger for emergency release from the whale's jaws!

As for the vault's other inmates…The overweight teenager was annoying, but only a pawn in the game that the fat so-called private detective, Morgan, had ridiculously twisted into tortured resemblance to a so-called "locked-room murrrderrr mystery". The kid had only followed the clown's's convoluted cue by suggesting the vault might contain a "secret compartment", which hinted that, say, a certain former VP of the Pioneer Bank might have hidden himself inside the vault before and after "murrrderrring" Old Man Black.

"See, Mr. Max," the overweight young Tweedle Dee was now saying to the older lookalike Tweedle Dum, "when Major McGrew used this first set of keys numbered 6167431 to open the box containing the first music-box monkey, and heard the tune of an old army barracks song beginning ♪This is number one and the fun has just begun… ♫"

"Yeah, it took Yours Truly a New York minute to dope out that last digits on the keys went 1-2-3 etcetera. Listen and learn, kid: keys are useless for combination-lock gizmos like the one stuck on the vault wall."

"Yeah, but when Major McGrew opened the second box with the matching key numbered 6943892, and sang the second song verse begining ♫This is number two and my hand is on her shoe...♫

George tuned out the nonsensical chatter, but...Hmmm. Come to think of it, what was up with the Mayor putting the so-called private detective and his teenaged assistant on the so-called escape team? Had Bailey baited him into a trap? Were the Mayor and the Chief of Police—sitting at the head table like judge-and-jury—hoping he would crack under pressure of confinement and suspicion; maybe blurt something incriminating about involvement in Black's death?

"So the second song verse may be a clue for the second digit following the beginning 6 common to all keys and boxes, which could be the second number of the emergency escape combination!"

"Yeah, but you said the second number to housing the 6 on the second key was a 4, not a 2. So no dice, kid, your musical hunch is 'off-key'."

Wondering if Gladys Black might have a half-pint of "courage" stashed in her canvas tote, George had an urge to crawl over to her, but... No, the old battleaxe was as much or more to blame than anyone for all that happened. Her constant nagging at Wild Bill to produce more and more financial support for her illusions of social grandeur, coupled with her steady physical decline into skin-and-bone uglier appearance...Hell, the single consolation for getting stuck in the stupid escape-room game was seeing Gladys Black reduced to obvious poverty, and obvious bitterness that her spouse was an incorrigible womanizer who...

George, after years of sobriety, felt like he was sinking back into dreaded DTs.

Struggling to get a grip on himself...Okay, Janie was, young and, uh, flirtatious by nature, but...Damnit, they were engaged to be married. She was not dumb, far from it. And the vault had always had thirty-nine safe deposit boxes. There was no need for an "inventory" to "re-calcuate" their number. So why did she go into the vault with Wild Bill, and let the old lecher lock the door behind them…a half-hour before the so-called robbery got underway?

George got a grip.

Yeah, it all added up: the undeserved promotion, the gold bracelet, the safe-deposit-box "inventory". And marriage counseling, what a joke! After four years of unhappy wedlock, the wife was trying to get rid of him. Probably she was in on Bailey's plot to pin Bill Black's death on him. Instead of sweeping mutual suspicion and distrust under a rug and going ahead with wary wedlock…Hell, it would have been a happier ever-after to their relationship if Janie Feinstein had not been rescued before oxygen inside the vault ran out!

George loosened his grip.

Okay, maybe he was paranoid, like Janie and the marriage counselor had been telling him. But like someone was said to have astutely observed: just because a guy was paranoid did not necessarily mean everyone was not out to get him.

"The first number after the 6 on the first key is a 1 alright," Higgs confirmed. "But yes, the second number after the 6 on the second key is indeed a 4, not a 2 that would have again mistakenly suggested an unlikely emergency unlocking combination of 1-2-3-4-5-6. So .. "

"And the third number after 6 etched on the third key to the third safe deposit box is a 7," said the junior private dick.

"Hmmm, let's see…the fourth number after 6 on the fourth key is a 2."

George, feeling lightheaded, heard possibly himself sing: ♫This is number four and her husband's at the door/ Roll me over in the clover and do it again…♫

"Okay, 1-4-7-2-2…" he heard Morgan say.

♫This is number six and I'm in an awful fix…♫

"Where in hell is the sixth key?!" he heard McGrew bark.

"Here it is!" he heard Gladys Black cry out.

"Okay, Jackson, gimme a read-out of the last digit on that last key. Loud and clear, soldier! TNT!"

"ZERO!"

With a mournful sigh, George accepted his impending fate.

"FUBAR!"

CHAPTER TWELVE

As seconds inched along like annoyed customers lined up at the Walmart customer complaints counter, Max sensed walls closing in…felt a ceiling bearing down on him…imagined water from an overflowing toilet rising on the floor…and a bathroom door locked from the other side. *Case of Locked in the Loo* was "fubar", but…

With a start, he came to his senses…found himself still locked inside the inescapable bank vault and…yet again checked his watch. The jig was up. With the game past thirty minutes into overtime and the old vault door likely unopenable from the outside, he gave up hope of rescue… staggered to the steel table…found a receipt from Harvey Brown's tire and muffler shop in a pants pocket…retrieved a ballpoint pen from a jacket pocket…put paper and pen on the table, and waved to his young "Watson".

He would tell the kid to jot that in the a.m. of May 14, 2025 Yours Truly was at his desk inside a Mister Quickie copy shop workstation cubicle, grappling with a head scratcher. On the blower, a joker manning a so-called help line had put him wise to…

"Re-dial 1-4-7-2-2-1—minus one—into the gizmo for emergency escape!" he shouted. But…

"There are no safe deposit box numbers ending in a zero," George McDonald mumbled.

The ex-bank VP, still slumped onto the vault floor, looked and sounded like he'd been on the gargle, but had inside info and…

"No ten, no twenty, no thirty, and…Unless Black had an off-the-books box for stashing loot from that so-called robbery five years ago—probably along with other ill-gotten funds—there would be no box numbered 40. Just like the old bastard to…"

"There's another ring of keys on the floor over here!" the Widow Black shrieked. "Dial in its last number!"

The kid scooped up the seventh pair of keys and started across the vault toward McGrew, shouting: "These are the keys for box number 6031736!"

Max intercepted the teenaged wannabe…grabbed the numerical clues…pushed McGrew aside…and took a deep breath.

"Here goes nothing," he muttered, before re-dialing right to 1- then left to 4 -then right to 7 again left to 2 again right to 2 …then left to a 6 at the end of the six-digit combination that would hopefully unlock…

Bingo!

The vault door swung open. Like a dam had broke, fresh air from the old banking hall flooded into the vault… along with a loud blast of banjo picking and…

♫**There's a big ol' hole/ right through the sole of this old shoe/ And the water on the ground ain't got no place it found/ So it's got one thing left to do…** ♫

What the heck! Mayor Bailey and the partygoers looked to have forgot all about the game part of the Fun-'n'-Game event.

♫**Creep on in/ Creep on in/ And once you have begun/ don't stop until you're done, sneakin' in** ♫

Rah! Rah! Rah!…

"Parade formation on the double, soldiers!" McGrew bellowed. "Fall in, look smart, and follow me!"

The retired National Guard officer adjusted his dented helmet, pushed Yours Truly aside and marched through the opened vault doorway, singing: ♫This is number six and I'm out of an awful fix… ♫

With his chest puffed up, Leroy Higgs marched behind the currently-employed Walmart customer complaint-counter clerk, singing way off-key: ♫This is number eight and we're finally out the gate... ♫

George McDonald got to his feet and joined the parade, croaking: ♫This is number nine and now I'm feeling fine... ♫

♫Roll us o-o-ver in the clo-o-over... ♫ even the kid, dog-gone-it, musically joined in, but...

Thankfully, banjo picking inside the banking hall drowned out the annoying march tune, and...

Rah! Rah! Rah!...

"Make yourself useful by helping me get out of here, you hopeless bungler!" the understandably cranky Widow Black shouted from her collapsed position.

♫**I had a friend named Ramlin' Bob/ He used to steal, gamble and rob/ He thought he was the smartest guy around...** ♫

Max helped the poor old widow to her feet.

♫**But I found out last Monday/ Bob got locked up Sunday...** ♫

With one bony hand clutching his elbow and the other clutching her canvas tote to her chest, the widow lurched toward the round vault doorway, and...

♫**Then I went out last Tuesday/ I met a gal named Susie...** ♫

Hello. A large wad of cash rolled in a rubber band fell out of the old broad's bag...then another wad dropped...and another.

♫**She started into calling me honey/ She started into spending my money...** ♫

Yeah, obviously the Missus Black had been in the know, if not in cahoots with the late Pioneer Bank boss stashing ninety-grand supposedly heisted in the bank robbery five years ago, and....

♫**We're in the jailhouse now** ♫

...might have finished off her spouse after finding him in throes of a heart attack inside the vault, while also — according to grapevine skinny — *en fragrante* with a young dame.

"Let go of me, you clumsy fool!" she now growled. "Your bungling has served its purpose."

The so-called escape-room game had been rigged alright. The real name of the game was Grand Larceny.

♫**We were countin' all the money** ♫ a Bushwhacker Boy

had changed to singing in the background as Max gripped the suspect's elbow and led her into the banking hall.

Rah! Rah! Rah!…

♫**We were smokin' stolen Marlboro Lights…** ♫

With the staged bank robbery and Wild Bill Black's death five years in the rearview mirror, the DA probably wouldn't have the goods to make a case for murrrderrr, or even nail the widow for cahoots in embezzlement of bank funds. But…

♫**Lord, we never saw 'em comin'/ 'Til they read us both our rights…** ♫

Likely ending up inside another locked room at the Iron Bars Hotel for re-stealing, the Widow Black would wise-up that she'd made a big mistake by likely arranging the escape-room game and inviting Yours Truly to come in and play.

Yeah, Gladys Black had orchestrated her semi-surreptitious return to the bank's abandoned safe-deposit-boxes vault before the old building got torn down, but—probably in confused panic during the game—had carelessly first handed over a seventh key to a box number ending 40 after stuffing its ill-gotten contents into her ratty canvas bag.

♫**With a sheriff right beside me/ Pistol pointed at my side…** ♫

In other words, Yours Truly's hunch had been almost right on the money. *Case of an Escape Room Escapade* had turned out to be a classic, but half-baked locked-room mystery alright, not so much about someone getting out of, but getting into the vault.

♫**Oh Lord, such a disappointing ending/ For a modern day Bonnie and Clyde** ♫

Rah! Rah! Rah!…

THE
END

CAT IN THE CRADLE

(and a silver spoon)

A Maximo Morgan Mystery

JUNE

WILLIAM LEROY

M
P Mossik Press

CAT IN THE CRADLE

(and a silver spoon)

A Maximo Morgan Mystery

JUNE

WILLIAM LEROY

TUESDAY

June 10, 2025

CHAPTER ONE

♫*Some folks are born, silver spoon in hand/ Lord, don't they help themselves, yeah...* ♫

With a tune from the Vietnam War era playing inside his head, Max sat at his regular Mister Quickie copy shop workstation, oiling a vintage U.S. Army service revolver with a rag. He'd heard that a famous oldtime Russian who jotted crime reports — *Case of The Shooting Party* and *Case of The Murder*, for instance — said a gun mentioned at the start of a report had to come into play in the finale. Yours Truly, however, was not prepping the old military weapon for action. He currently had no lay to work, and his Unarmed P.I. License barely allowed him to pack his exact replica of Mike Hammer's "Old Junior" that didn't actually squirt lead.

The vintage U.S. Army sidearm in hand was a treasured "remembrance" of the long-deceased father he otherwise did not remember and, in effect, a silver spoon of sorts.

♫*It ain't me, it ain't me/ I ain't no millionaire's son, Son...* ♫

There was no military draft when he came of age. And his weight, pear-shaped physique, plus flat feet had ruled out Army enlistment, but...

♫*And when the Band plays "Hail to the Chief"/ They point the gun at you, Lord...* ♫

Yours Truly had carried on a family tradition of serving in uniform. For almost thirteen years he had marched over hill-and-dale in rain, snow, heat and gloom of night for the United States Postal Service. For almost another thirteen years he had manned the post office sorting room, fending off constant attack by hostile customers. Now retired from duty, yeah, he still had a key to the post office back door, but almost all his buddies had also bit a bullet. He missed the feeling of belonging to a tight group of brothers-in-arms.

♪*It ain't me, it ain't me/I ain't no fortunate son, Son...* ♪

In particular, he missed hanging out with pals in the post office Rubber Room...taking breaks to relieve stress...letting off steam...shooting breeze...telling "war stories"...trying to keep from "going postal" and...

A shadow appeared on the desk surface. Max looked up. Hovering above him...

"'Maximo Morgan' ..." said a tall, semi-dark-skinned joker, standing there in a white bathrobe with a towel strapped onto his head. "'Discreet Private Investigations'...'Confidentiality Guaranteed'...'Notary Public'...?" the walk-in said, scratching his black beard as he looked down at the three desk plaques that he'd read aloud.

"Yeah, Maximo Morgan by name, private dicking by game," Max confirmed. "Stamping documents is Yours Truly's sideline. Which will it be, Mr.... ?"

"Call me Ishmael Ben Ahab," said the foreign-looking but English-speaking stranger, before seating himself in the client chair across the desk. "I require very confidential services to find a woman living in this area twenty-five years ago. Yes, better to sleep with a cannibal than a drunk Christian. But here I am, product of my father's seed. See how elastic our prejudices grow when once lust comes to bend them."

In somewhat plainer English-speaking, the youngish Ishmael Ben Ahab —likely of Arab heritage—explained that he had been raised by his father, sure enough "in the land of the burning sand", and needed professional assistance to find a person he referred to as a "she" briefly known by his old man.

"Who's 'she', the cat's mother?" said Max, echoing his mom's disapproval of impersonal and, in her view, disrespectful references to women, including moms in particular.

"She is in fact the person who birthed me," said the would-be client. "My father identified her only as a 'Qareen'."

In other words: a run-of-the-mill domestic relations lay likely not worth the paper-and-pencil lead of a jotted case report, but…

Hmmm.

Hercule Poirot's *Case of the Adventures of Johnny Waverly* came to mind, a not very interesting "adventure" in which a man staged the kidnapping of his own three-year-old son in a plot to squeeze cash from the boy's wealthy mother, supposedly for "payment of ransom".

Hmmm.

Max also recalled that Sam Spade's first lay after setting up shop in Frisco had been to track down the missing son of a wealthy banker.

Hmmm.

And yeah, a following Spade case had kicked off with the seemingly innocent "Ruth Wonderly"—a/k/a the infamous *femme fatale*, Brigid O'Shaughnessy—ankling into his office and hiring Sam to find a missing sister who…Bingo. Spade found himself entangled in a web of *noirish* intrigue in *Case of the Maltese Falcon* that made him famous.

In other words, though off-put by Ahab's cold attitude toward his maternal matter, a lay of tracking down a mysterious mom might have case report jotting and publication possibilities as *Case of the Cat's Mother.*

CHAPTER TWO

♫**Privates, they love their beer, three times a day/ Corporals, they love their stripes, and that ain't hay...** ♫

Inside the local VFW Hall, G.I. "Trans" Porter silently moved her lips as other members of the Veterans of Foreign Wars Post 539 boisterously sang an apt old-boys barracks song, led by the post's Judge Advocate, a clown named Roger "Dodger" Madison.

♫**Sergeants put you through the mill/ They just drill and drill and drill, until they fade away...** ♫

While others in attendance wore only the standard VFW black garrison cap appropriately emblazoned to signify post affiliation, Madison wore a red cap with gold tassels—turned sideways and looking more like a fez than American military issue—and adorned with bug insignia to ostentatiously broadcast his affiliation with a sub-auxiliary unit known as the Military Order of the Cooties.

♫**Old soldiers never die/ Old soldiers never die/ They just fade away/ They just fade away...** ♫

Cooties boasted of being an elite corps within the VFW dating back to the 1920s, when World War I veterans memorialized their survival by crediting the need to scratch lice for them keeping their heads down in trenches. Their units were called "Pup Tents". Their separate meetings were called "scratches'". Their mission—as formally stated in the Preamble of MOC By-Laws—was "to have fun". And in that regard, though none other, Dodger Madison was known for doing his duty on virtually a daily basis at the VFW Hall's bar.

♫**Washington, Grant and Lee were all tried and true/**

Eisenhower, Bradley. MacArthur too/ They will live forevermore, 'til the world is done with war/ Then they'll close that final door, and fade away... ♫

Unfortunately, "fading nicely", as memorably put by a limp-wristed newspaper writer following General MacArthur's unceremonious firing during the Korean War. And the same had been true of VFW membership dating back to the organization's initial refusal to recognize that vets of the undeclared Vietnam War had "served on hostile soil, in hostile waters or the airspace above." Though the egregious error was corrected years following the ignominious end of the war, VFW membership had "faded" in droves before somewhat rebounding to its current national level of only about one million national dues payers.

G.I. herself—called "Trans" dating back to her service in the U.S. Army Transportation Corps—had been a Humvee driver for two-and-a-half tours of duty in Iraq and Afghanistan before being mustered out. If not for running over a IED and taking a blast "up the kazoo", she would have remained a proud U.S. Army active-duty soldier until...

♫Old soldiers never die/ Never die/ Old soldiers never die/ They just fade away ♫

Tap. Tap.

"That was fun," said Commander Bud "Butt Crack" McCracken—a plumber by vocation—after tapping a gavel on a podium set on a bandstand. "Takes me back to beer busts down at Fort Polk."

"Hear! Hear!" added Adjutant Irwin "Win Win" Williams—a used car salesman-before taking his seat to the Commander's right. "Good show, Dodger."

"Don't you dare 'fade away', Dodger," said Quartermaster Charlie Mike Wilcox—a Walmart clerk—on the Commander's left. "Not 'til you settle your bar tab."

Ha, ha, ha, ha, ha....

"Dodger's too ornery to die," Chaplain Ray Ray "X-Ray" Watkins announced, which, unfortunately, was probably true.

Ha, ha, ha, ha, ha...

"Who goes there?!" G.I. then shouted in her capacity as Sergeant-of-the-Guard.

"Who invited hookers? Haw, haw, haw…"

Though in fact no one had actually knocked, by pre-arrangement G.I. opened a door.

"Conductress Felix from the VFW Auxiliary requests permission to speak," said Barbara Felix — a hairdresser — stepping into the hall and, as also pre-arranged, moving into position at the portable altar facing Commander McCracken.

The Conductress, an officer of the VFW Auxiliary charged with making arrangements for her group's meetings, was a chronic grouser about Auxiliary members' rightful status as "second class citizens". And though not pre-arranged, sure enough…

"This is our home too," she said, to begin a likely litany of complaints. "I don't want to be a nag, but boys, boys, boys, let's watch the cigarette butts, okay? And you know what glasses on tables do."

"They get emptied," Dodger Madison shouted. "Haw, haw, haw …"

"They leave rings on the tables that…"

"Better than a wife's ring in my nose! Haw, haw, haw…"

"Is it too much to ask that you use the coasters provided by the Auxiliary? Do you want to socialize in a pigsty?"

G.I. deplored sissification of Post 539. For almost a hundred years of its history the VFW Auxiliary had been for split-tails only, and was still dominated by females though increasing in mixed membership. On the other hand, fellow members of the VFW proper — almost all males — had turned the hall into a virtual honky-tonk. Last week, for instance, who else but Dodger Madison had entertained two female guests of obvious tawdry character at the bar, got knee-walking drunk himself, and further defiled the premises by…

Tap. Tap.

"We've been through these, uh, housekeeping issues before, Conductress Felix," said the Commander. "The meeting is now open for only new business of immediate importance."

The Auxiliary emissary apologized for short notice, then requested exclusive use of the hall tomorrow for election and initiation of new Auxiliary members.

G.I. ground her teeth. Membership in the VFW Auxiliary required only that a person be the parent, grandparent, spouse, sibling, child or grandchild of a veteran qualified for VFW membership. So nowadays Auxilary chickenhawks marched in parades while too many real veterans stood by and watched with disgust.

Obviously likewise annoyed, the Commander directed a stink-eye in the direction of Dodger Madison, the glad-hander supposedly in charge of VFW recruitment who had not reeled in a new member since "Pap" was in the Army, so to speak.

"Any chance any of your recruits would qualify for bona fide VFW membership, Conductor Felix?" Commander Butt Crack asked, with a pathetic pleading look in his eyes. "Who have you lined up?"

"No actual veterans are among the applicants we will vote on and expect to initiate tomorrow," the Auxiliary officer reported, taking a sheet of paper from a purse! "The four current candidates for membership include:

"Ms. Bertha Bigelow, widow of U.S. Army Staff Sergeant Charles Bigelow, deceased.

"Ms. Fredda Dean, mother of US. Army Corporal Matthew Dean, inactive reservist.

"Ms. Beatrice Ward, daughter of U.S. Air Force Major Brian Ward, retired.

"Mr. Maxwell Morgan, son of U.S. Army Sergeant Homer Morgan, deceased."

"All have submitted paperwork for membership and…"

"Objection to Max Morgan!" G.I. blurted.

"On what grounds, Sergeant-of-the-Guard?"

"On multiple grounds, Commander."

"Technically, an Auxiliary matter, but…"

"Morgan was my family's mailman for years, and mishandled and/or lost countless letters containing my daddy's VA benefits.

Moved to the post office sorting room, he was seen peeking into and/or sniffing the contents of packages marked 'Personal'. And...And...Picture the fat mailman in *Seinfeld*. Do you want to see a 'Neumann' marching with us in parades? He would be a disgrace to VFW and Auxiliary caps."

"The Sergeant-of-the-Guard makes a good point," said Dodger Madison. "Max Morgan is around fifty, still lives with his mother, and is a tee-totaler. He's no fun."

"Thought of Max Morgan's presence in this hall makes me want to...Well, suffice it to say that if Morgan is elected to VFW Auxiliary membership, I for one will never again set foot on these premises!" G.I. declared.

"Hmmm," Madison hmmmed. "On the other hand, Max is a Notary Public, and would be handy to have around."

"And he's now also a private investigator," said "Win Win" Williams, the ass kisser. "If he gets rejected...Well, 'stead of having him outside the tent, peeking in, it might be better to have him on the inside."

G.I. was appalled, and then some, that a doofus such as Max Morgan would be considered for membership in the Veterans of Foreign Wars affiliate. The America she had sacrificed body parts for was the America that honored personnel of demonstrated merit, not slackers privileged to have been simply born to a military parent without risk to life, limb and kazoo.

CHAPTER THREE

Max parked his mom's brown Buick boiler in the Saint Michael's Church lot, got out of the ride, and ankled beneath an exposed-steel bell tower toward the A-frame church building.

Saint Michael's, and in particular its longtime boss man, Father Vincente Quesada, had long histories of coming to the aid of abandoned mothers. And Yours Truly was tight with the padre, a former client. Last year—suspicious that a mysterious "jigger man" was responsible for stirring up teenaged gang activity centered in the semi-wild and abandoned hogback area west of town—Father Vincente had hired him to identify the "satanic puppeteer". Turned out "Satan" was the local millionaire, Jonathan Henry, whose plot was to get the hogback declared a public nuisance that the town would sell to him for development. But...

"Oh, it's you," said the old, silver-haired priest, standing inside the church vestibule, washing his hands at a basin. High-priced mansions were now being built on and around the hogback instead of affordable housing. And gang activity had relocated to the padre's part of town, probably disappointing the old bead-counter. But...

"Got a client who's searching for his birth mother," said Max. "Working on a hunch that she might have been part of your flock back in 2000-2001. Known only as 'Qareen' by the client's birth father who came through these parts back then."

"And what is the son's name?" said the old man of cloth, with a semi-knowing look in his shifty eyes.

"Confidential poop, Padre. But just between us chickens, so to speak, the client goes by 'Ishmael Benjamin Ahab'. An Arab, by the look of him. Raised by his old man in a land of the burning sun."

"Raised as a Muslim?"

"Couldn't say. He wears camel-jockey clothes, but didn't mention religion."

"Why does 'Mr. Ahab the Arab' want to find his birth mother after all these years? What does he want of her? 'Hugs-and-kisses'? 'Homemade pie'? Or something else?"

Max was stumped by the questions, so simple that he had not bothered to put them to the client.

"Wait here," said the holy father figure, before turning away and disappearing through a side door.

While cooling his heels, Max had a feeling he was already getting warm, but…Why did Ahab the Arab come all the way from a land of burning sand to find the mother he'd never known?

Hmmm.

At the request of his own mom, he had visited a shrink on a few occasions — a Dr. Gloria Stern — who had quoted a Dr. Sigmund Freud to the effect that separation from a mother by birth itself was the central trauma of life experienced by supposedly everyone. Not Yours Truly. He had lived his whole life with his mom in the house where he was born. His trauma — again according to Stern — was supposedly competition with his father for food when he was a toddler that, coupled with his old man's death, had given him a so-called "Edible Complex" that made him feel guilty about eating, say, pie.

Hmmm.

The "trauma" experienced by a buddy back in his post office sorting room days came to mind. Barney Smithers had been raised by adoptive parents and had no complaints about his upbringing, but at the age of forty got an itch to identify and look up his birth mother. Just curiosity, he'd said. But after locating and paying an unannounced visit to his maternal flesh-and-blood in California, he'd retreated almost daily for almost all-day breaks in the post office Rubber Room. Not due to aroused feelings of "rejection, abandonment, grief, shame, and guilt," as suggested by a USPS counselor. Barney had been traumatized by discovery that his natural mother and half-siblings all had lumps on their necks called goiters.

Had Ahab considered the risk of finding that he too was by birth susceptible to hereditary…?

The side door opened and Father Vincente came through with a dark look on his semi-dark-skinned face.

"I have spoken to the woman who likely gave birth to your client on April 15, 2000," he said. "Against my strong advice, she has agreed to be, uh, reunited with her son. I shall insist on being present, but responsibility for any resulting trauma shall be upon you, Maxwell Morgan."

Uh oh. Did the client's birth mother, now into her early forties at least, display any, uh, undesirable genetic traits?

"She is a lovely woman, badly used and abused by Mr. Ahab's father, who accused her of 'trickery' and…Her name is Carlita, not 'Qareen', which is what a legendary demonic woman in Islamic lore is called."

Lovely demonic woman! The old man of cloth was not an old man of the world who would know a tricky *femme fatale* from a fair-haired frail. And now an onus—like one of those albatross birds netted by accident in an ancient book assigned during high school—was hanging on Yours Truly's neck like a goiter, and might turn out to be a curse.

"Heaven help us," said Quesada, crossing himself. "Let us pray: Saint Michael, the Archangel, be thy humble servant's defense against the wickedness and snares of the Devil. May God rebuke the Evil One, we pray. Amen."

"Amen!"

CHAPTER FOUR

♫*All-American boy, with a silver spoon/ His future held all the promise of a president/ Wonder where it went...* ♫

With wall-mounted photos of his grandfather and father hovering over him like Old Testament patriarchs and Waylon Jennings wailing in the background of his mind, Mayor Buford Bailey sat slumped at his Bailey Insurance Agency desk, feeling like Joe Biden must have felt during the ex-President's last days in office. After a lifetime of public service, including twenty-five years as Mayor, he had fallen out of favor with voters. A recall petition had effectively put him up for re-re-election that he was bound to lose. And worst of all, his legacy would amount to nothing worth being written about on paper, much less etched on a stone pedestal of a lasting monument.

♫*It's hard to be the crowned prince when it all hits home/ You can't hide behind the wall around the throne...* ♫

Because his grandfather and father before him had been popular Mayors and successful independent insurance agents, he'd never got credit for his own accomplishments. That was the downside to being the beneficiary of a legacy. He'd been born with a silver spoon in his mouth, people said. He'd been born on third base and thought he'd hit a triple, a political opponent had taunted in support of the recall petition. But darn it, he had not chosen to follow in parental and grandparental footsteps. He had been "typecast".

In grade school, because he was the son and grandson of Mayors, teachers had always assigned to him the honor of leading recital of the Pledge of Allegiance. In high school, because he was the presumed heir of the Bailey Insurance Agency—and carried his books in a briefcase—he had been repeatedly elected to serve as both class president and secretary/ treasurer.

Buford sighed. He couldn't credibly claim that demands of other responsibilities had kept him from realizing his ambition to become a Grand Old Opry rock star. He'd been born without a knack for singing, for playing a musical instrument, for even tapping his toes in the rhythm of a song such as...

♪ *The real world's not a playground, it's a danger zone/ You find out who you really are when the pressure's on...* ♪

Unlike other young men, he'd dropped out of Murray State Junior College down in Tishomingo after a single semester, not because he'd had to get married or even had a hometown girlfriend...not because he'd wanted to join the Navy, so to speak, and see the world...and not because he'd needed to earn a living. He had been lured to take his appointed place in a warm tub of butter, so to speak, available to him by way of what people used to call membership in a political "dynasty", and now criticized as a system of nepotism. Just as voters had tired of Bush family members...

♪*It's hard to be a crowned prince when it all hits home...* ♪

He'd had no time for marriage and children. He'd dedicated his life to public service and carrying on a family business. When he was gone...Though now painful to contemplate, he had long since bought a burial plot for himself, and put in place a large stone monument with the date of his passing left blank along with plenty of room for fitting words of remembrance that he had already composed on paper, beginning: "Here lies a man who could talk with crowds but keep his virtue, and walk with kings and queens, nor lose the common touch..."

But dog-gone-it, his announcement of a donation of papers and memorabilia for addition of a Buford P. Bailey wing to the public library had fallen flat. That Hispanic town councilwoman opposing him in the upcoming mayoral run-off—Ms. Obrador-Cortez—had proposed that the Buford P. Bailey Park be decommissioned and paved over to provide for sanitation truck parking. And his longtime pet project...

♫ *When it all hits home/ You can't hide behind the wall around the throne...* ♫

Buford again sighed. Eleven years ago, he'd pushed through a town bond issue to finance putting a golf course in the area surrounding a large hogback hill west of town. To tee up development of high-priced houses on the hogback, he had promoted a major golf tournament. But lightning had set the bushy hill on fire, the tournament had been a fiasco, and a goofy local do-gooder had got the federal government to declare the area a nature preserve for an endangered breed of mayflies. Thankfully, all that had been forgotten by voters until three months ago, when...

Without a respectful knock, the door to his office opened. In came the agency's longtime office manager, Marilyn Hopping, followed by...

"I apologize for interrupting your, uh, noodling, Buford," said Ms. Hopping, "but Mr. Dean insists..."

"Damnit, Bufie, your father and grandfather would be rolling over in their graves if they were alive today," Old Man Dean shouted. "But you'll pay for the losses, by God, no matter what that 'force of manure' clause in my policy says."

The irate longtime agency client went on to complain that under what must have been a "force majeure" clause of his policy—excluding coverage for losses caused by acts of God—the Regressive Insurance Company was refusing to pay for loss-and-damage to eight rental sheds and contents resulting from the rain, wind and flooding brought by a major storm last spring.

Buford looked to Ms. Hopping, who then left the office, no doubt to fetch the Dean file. He himself had always operated as more of a ship's captain than hands-on proprietor of the inherited business. The bulk of agency revenue was generated by routine renewals of pre-existing policies, most dating back to his father's time at the helm, some dating back to his grandfather's seamanship. Ms. Hopping had always handled the paperwork, while he…

"How's the family?" Buford asked, rolling dice, so to speak, that there was still a Dean family to inquire about.

"Not so damned good," came the disgruntled customer's reply. "The wife slipped in mud while trying to salvage some family hairlooms from the flood, cut her foot and got an infection. But damnit, you bundled, or rather bungled all our policies, and now those Regressive sumbitches are saying loss of toes are not covered by our so-called health insurance, and are part of the flood losses that exclude…"

"Here it is," said Ms. Hopping, waddling back into the office with an opened folder in hand. "To partially off-set an increase in premiums, Mr. Dean, you opted for Regressive's affordable 'Onus-on-You Plan' that clearly excludes coverage of losses caused by force majeure—extraordinary events sometimes referred to as acts of God—expressly including 'rain, wind and flooding'. It's all spelled out in the fine print."

"Why, for God's sake, would anyone pay for insurance to cover the very risks of loss excluded from coverage under that… that fine print?"

"Don't blame Ms. Hopping," said Buford, before venturing to explain that costs of replacing storage sheds and contents had no doubt increased due to inflation during Biden's term in office, not to mention foot doctor fees.

"I blame your greed, Bufie," said the self-entitled old codger. "And one way or another I'm going to have a pound of your sorry ass to make up for loss of the wife's toes!"

Left to himself, Buford remained on edge.

Damnit, that homicidal maniac, Luigi Mangeone, and his media accomplices had convinced everyone that insurance was not a business, but a charity funded by someone other than themselves. Totally lost in left-wing media accounts of Mangione's coldblooded murder of a "greedy" United Healthcare Insurance Company executive was that following its devastating losses incurred during the Covid pandemic, United Healthcare's return on costs had been less than 5%. Health care in the

U.S.A. itself—costing twice as much as in other developed countries—was the true villain. If anything, doctors should be gunned down, not...not....

Magione, an over-privileged Ivy League punk, was now a celebrated folk hero to many, while the forgotten "villainous" victim of his crime might as well have been nameless.

Buford yet again sighed.

After being left for dead, his pet project—development of the hogback area—had been revived when the feds declared the previously endangered breed of mayflies to be extinct and a local big shot put in a bid to build high-priced houses lining a new golf course on the property. But...Dang it, the project had become controversial, and he—faced with left-wing rabble-rousing roused by Ms. Obrador-Cortez—had, uh, modified his position. Now the project that had been his baby was moving ahead. But for the major civic improvement that coulda, shoulda and woulda been his legacy, he was on record as having opposed it. Yeah...

♫*The real world's not a playground, it's a danger zone/ And when the pressure is on...* ♫

Again without a respectful knock, the door to his office again opened. Again, in came Ms. Hopping, carrying not a folder but her oversized handbag.

"Buford, I started working here when your father was in charge," she said. "For thirty years since then I have done my best to keep things afloat, but...The ship is sinking, Buford. You're on your own."

On his own? For crying out loud, he was, uh, captain of the ship only by inheritance and.... Buford looked up to the wall-mounted photo of his grandfather, Buford Bailey the First...to the photo of his father, Buford Bailey, Junior....and to the photo of...

♫*He's the first one in his family to wind up second best/ He couldn't pass the test...* ♫

He had stopped referring to himself as 'the Third" after the wisecracking father of a high school friend had used a fake

Brooklyn accent to make "Third" sound like "toid". And now...
♫*Where life begins or where it ends/ It all depends*♫

CHAPTER FIVE

Basking in his mom's beaming approval, Max nevertheless felt a tad undeserving of the fried chicken dinner she had stood over a skillet of hot grease to fix for him. Cracking *Case of the Cat's Mother* had been a good deed that took private dick know-how, but…He felt somewhat guilty about the grand he would have coming to him for so easily locating the woman the client had referred to as a "birthing person". And a little nervous about the onus of re-connecting them. But his mom . .

"No doubt your client's father kidnapped his infant son and took the child to a 'land of burning sand' against the poor mother's will," Mom said, putting a fresh-baked cherry pie on the kitchen table. "If she had tried to rescue the little one, well, you know what happened in *Case of Not With My Daughter*."

Yeah, Yours Truly was wise to what went down in the famous case of a birth father taking his American wife and daughter to the land of Iran, supposedly for a brief visit to meet his family… signing up the kid for Muslim Sunday School…confining and beating the wife…and refusing to let the birth mother take the little one back to their United States homeland. When the mom sneaked into an embassy to get help, she was told that she had become an Iranian citizen by marriage and her daughter by birth…and that they were stuck. But…

Dang it, his own mom had never had a daughter, had not read his deceased father's pulp case reports stashed in the attic, and was not able to see that young dames, even as teenagers, could be *femmes fatale*. For all Mom knew, "Carlita" was in fact a "Qareen" who had pegged Ishmael's young old man as a good catch, and attempted to trap him in wedlock by hanging an albatross bird around his neck.

"The mother-and-child connection, even if not exactly as one would have chosen, is the strongest in nature, Max, as you yourself should know."

Maybe so in most cases. Though his mom had hoped Yours Truly would be a girl—now a "Jessica Fletcher" of *Murder, She Wrote* fame instead of a less famous "Brad Runyon" a/k/a The Fat Man—they were close as two squirrels caught in a drain pipe. In other cases…Yours Truly was no fan of birth fathers *per se*. A sperm donor, known only as RR529 at the time, had come between him and a main squeeze named Trudy Berger a few years ago. But as a general matter, what made the layer of the egg more entitled to parenthood than the rooster?

"A child is carried by its mother inside her womb for the first, most important, most bonding experience of its life."

Yeah, but in *Case of the Cat's Mother*, put kindly, it may have been that Carlita Somebody was unable to take care of a newborn. Put less kindly, she may have took a pay-off to have an unwanted kid taken off her hands. Anyway, Yours Truly's client had come all the way from a land of burning sand, and was willing to pay a grand for…

Buzz. Buzz. Buzz.

Speak of the devil, so to speak, it was Ahab the Arab calling on the phone.

"Uh huh…Uh huh…Uh huh."

As instructed, Max ankled down the street for half-a-block and got into a black car occupied by the client.

Mindful to not make his gumshoeing sound undeserving of a thousand clams, he noted that the year 2000 was a long time ago.

"Twenty-five years," said young Ishmael. "I figured out that part myself."

People moved away or died, Max continued. Those with knowledge of unfortunate past events often refused to talk about the past. Especially without knowing…

"I don't recall you mentioning exactly why you are so het-up to find your birth mother, Ahab. What is it that you want…?"

"That's a private matter. What progress have you made?"

"Well, for one thing, you must have misheard your old man's reference to your, uh, birthing person. Her name is not 'Qareen'. It's…"

"Did you make contact? Did you confirm…?"

"Had to wear gum off the gumshoes, but yeah, your mother's name is Carlita and…"

"Carlita?! Is she dark-skinned? Is she Hispanic?"

"Couldn't say, sight unseen. But no mention of, say, goiters. She's agreeable to a face-to-face, but wants to know …"

"I have no desire to meet the infidel who served my father's carnal appetite, Mr. Morgan. You claim to be a *notario publico*. All I want is for you to establish is whether or not the Qareen is a citizen of the United States of America."

Aha. Mystery solved. To Ishmael Ben Ahab the Arab, his mother—though never married to his father—had effectively been a mail-order bride in reverse. Instead of importing an American woman to his land of the burning sand for marriage, the client's old man had come to the U.S. to hook-up with a "birthing person". What the client wanted from her was not a 'hug and pie", at least not exactly. He wanted citizenship in the U.S. of A. by maternal inheritance, which made Yours Truly…

Max had not liked the cut of Ahab's jib, as a tailor would say, and now felt sort of like an ICE agent on the take, if not an actual "coyote" of sorts, engaged in getting a foreigner past emigration checkpoints protecting the country from troublemakers.

WEDNESDAY

June 16, 2025

CHAPTER SIX

♫*My old man's that old man, spent his life livin' off the land/ It breaks his heart to see foreign cars, runnin' on gas that ain't ours...* ♫

At the desk inside a Mister Quickie copy shop workstation cubicle that served as his office, Max—figuratively speaking—crossed his fingers. His application for membership in the Veterans of Foreign Wars Auxiliary was scheduled for approval today.

♫*He's got the red, white, blue flag flyin' high on the farm/ Semper Fi tattooed on his left arm...* ♫

Barring hiccups, by this evening he would belong to the VFW Auxiliary... allowed to hang out with military veterans and other relatives of veterans at the VFW Hall bar...drinking root beer... letting off steam ...shooting breeze...swapping war stories...

♫*He ain't prejudiced, he's just Made in America...* ♫

But...Dang it, if that fussy VFW Conductress, Ms. Felix, found out he had been working—totally by accident—as a "coyote" of sorts for Ahab the Arab, and...

He opened his laptop and Googled *Notario Publico*, the foreign term that Ahab had seemed to make such a big deal about. On the computer screen, oh no, up came a headline: **About Notario Fraud,** followed by....

The term "notario publico" is particularly problematic in that it creates a unique opportunity for deception. The literal translation is "notary public".

Uh oh.

While a notary public in the United States is authorized only to witness the signature of forms, a notary public in many countries refers to an individual who has received the equivalent of a law license. The problem arises when individuals use that license to substantiate representations that they are a "notario publico" to immigrant populations that ascribe to a vastly different meaning of the term.

Dang it, as a licensed Notary he stamped documents for copy shop customers in return for Quickie allowing him to occupy the workstation cubicle on a full-time basis. But he'd done no stamping of Ahab the Arab's signature. And as a licensed private eye, all he'd done was track down the foreign client's local birth mother. Any fraud afoot was not his doing, but…Double-dang it, worse than possibly losing both his Notary and P.I. licenses, if that VFW Conductress got wind…

"Yo, Mr. Maximo," said the familiar voice of the teenaged kid who served as his case report jotter. "What's got you looking so sorta out of sorts?"

He had taken the also overweight, also pear-shaped wannabe private dick under a wing. As a role model and mentor, he had a responsibility to both pass on tricks of the gumshoe game and set a good example. But with *Case of the Cat's Mother* now having the smell of a citizenship scam he'd unwittingly stepped in…

Hmmm.

No need to disillusion the young protege by revealing Yours Truly's slip-up.

"Ready to jot when you are, Mr. Max."

On the other hand, the kid—like Sherlock Holmes' case report jotter, Doc Watson—occasionally provided useful feedback.

So after leaning back in his double-wide chair, Max put his own "Watson" wise. Bottom line: it looked like he would have to face music. To clear his name and remove a possible hickey on his VFW Auxiliary membership application, he would have to tell Ahab the Arab's abandoned, likely undocumented Mexican birth mother that her son's only interest in her was…

"Yeah, citizenship, it's a slippery slope according to our Civics Class teacher, Mr. Whitney," said the young jotter, now seated in the client chair with pad-and-pencil in hand. "For instance,

Jewish people born and living around the world have a right to Israeli citizenship just by being Jewish. Palestinian Arabs, on the other hand, though never members of any recognized independent nation, feel attached to and part of the land they and their ancestors have occupied over time, sorta like feudal serfs in the European middle ages."

"Very interesting," said Max, "but Ahab the Arab obviously does not feel 'attached' to his native land of the burning sand, and not to his mother except to establish a family relationship with Uncle Sam."

"Ancient Romans granted citizenship to peoples they conquered, mainly to justify required military service and/or payment of taxes as opposed to providing rights," the bookish kid continued. "And though the process is difficult, resident foreigners can become citizens of France, but people say applicants—unlike immigrants becoming Americans—can never really become 'Frenchmen'.

"And citizenship in Arab 'countries of the burning sand' such as Saudi Arabia are even more tangled according to my Uncle Ralph, the rabbi. For instance, in our client's case involving an American birth mother…"

"Also probably interesting, but also beside the point. Yours Truly's client only wants to be recognized as son of an American mother in order to cash-in on U.S. freebies available by way of inheritance."

"Yeah, that's just not right, Mr. Max. Heck, laws are being passed in the United States to stop elite colleges that get public funds from favoring applicants who are children of their alums. Legacy rights are unAmerican, if not unconstitutional."

Laws against legacies?

"Well, I wouldn't go that far," Max quibbled. "Working hard for something to pass on is the American way in Yours Truly's book." As was service in Uncle Sam's military, he silently noted, mindful that his membership in the Veterans of Foreign Wars elite club would be based on his father's stint in the U.S. Army.

"Our Social Studies teacher, Ms. Phlegming, thinks countries along with citizenship should be borderless, and genderless, by the way."

Genderless?

"Yeah, whereas Mr. Whitney says that thinking of countries as fatherland implies authority and nationality, and that the term motherland implies protective nurturing by a person's country of origin, Ms. Phlegming forbids us to use the terms father and mother. To Uncle Ralph, that implies currently existing nations should be called 'XYland' and 'XXland'."

"Get it, Mr. Max? 'XY' for paternal 'spermland' and 'XX' for maternal 'eggland'. Uncle Ralph is a jokester, but…What about the children of that Canadian guy in the documentary, 'Starbuck', who made over five hundred sperm donations that could've been shipped around the word? A kid born in, say, Mongolia to a Mongolian mother would be a citizen of Canada. So Uncle Ralph agrees with Ms. Phlegming in a bassackward way, and says everyone should have to pass a civics test—and make a pledge of allegiance—to become a country's citizen regardless of who their parents are or where…"

Finding the kid's feedback to be not particularly useful, Max returned to doping out whether the savvy play would be to quiz the client's birth mother about her citizenship without confiding her uncaring son's motive, or to just drop *Case of the Cat's Mother* and let dogs that had been sleeping for twenty-five years lie, without "barking", so to speak, at Conductress Felix. But…

"Anyway, no *problemo*, Mr. Max. The Fourteenth Amendment to the United States Constitution, adopted after slaves were freed by the Civil War, provides for automatic birthright citizenship of anyone born on American soil, despite lack of parental citizenship that had disqualified former slaves and their descendants."

Max could hardly believe his lucky break. If Ahab the Arab was automatically already a U.S. citizen there would be no hint of a scam. No harm, no foul. Yours Truly's application for VFW Auxiliary membership would be in the bag.

CHAPTER SEVEN

♫ *Take your silver spoon and dig your grave…* ♫

Plagued by another musical earworm planted years ago by Waylon Jennings, Buford—with a sigh—closed the Bailey Insurance Agency ledger. The longtime office manager, Marilyn Hopping, had tended to the record since before his time in charge of the family business. And yesterday, when confronted by Old Man Dean's complaint about his bundled policy's non-coverage of losses, the disloyal old biddy must have foreseen the book's predictable sad ending.

The Liberty Insurance Company—that used to imply it covered claims for losses denied by competitors—now more honestly advertised that "you get for what you pay for". Farmers Insurance Company, that used to brag on its "Hall of Claims", no longer ran commercials about how oddball losses—say, damages from a car wreck caused by a pet gerbil getting loose and crawling up a driver's pant leg—were covered because they had "seen a thing or two, and knew a thing or two". But…

Ms. Poppins had kept the Bailey agency afloat by processing routine renewals of policies with various companies that maintained reasonably unaffordable premiums for—in fine print—reduced coverage not including losses caused by, say, loose gerbils or even other drivers running red lights. And now chickens were coming home to roost. Yesterday's unpleasantness with Old Man Dean about uncovered loss of a few toes was only the latest in an upward trend of complaints. And as the old saying went: When you find yourself in a hole…

♫ *Take your silver spoon and dig your grave…* ♫

Feeling like B'rer Rabbit, stuck to a tar baby of sorts, Buford—with another sigh—got up from his desk, determined to stop digging his... hole.

At his office doorway, he looked back at the wall-mounted photos of his grandfather and father, both of whom seemed to return his gaze with expressions more disapproving than usual.

At the agency's front door, he posted a sign—OUT TO LUNCH—and exited the only workplace he had ever occupied.

Warily, he walked along Main Street of his hometown, on the lookout for armed thugs chanting that murderous Mangione mantra: "Deny! Delay! Defend!" But...Most of the mostly younger locals he encountered were strangers, not wearing *Free Luigi!* tee-shirts. No one, thankfully, seemed to recognize him as the town's longtime Mayor, tarred by his radical political opponent as an "insurance agent".

Contrary to years of past practice, he didn't dare introduce himself, extend a hand, and ask for votes in the upcoming unelection. Not that it mattered. He was almost certain to be booted from office.

♫*Take your silver spoon and dig your grave...* ♫

At the corner of Tenth Street and Main—intent on convincing a "Brer Bear" to help him get out of a hole and into a safe briar patch—Buford entered the office of a newly established Allstate Insurance Agency.

The "good hands people" themselves, while warning about lousy coverage provided by cut-rate insurance companies for losses caused by "Mister Mayhem", owned and operated such companies under different names. They too knew a few things, and...

"Sorry, Mayor Bailey," said young Joe Bob Baker, Jr. "The boss doesn't allow panhandling or solicitations on the premises."

Having already stopped wearing a VOTE FOR BAILEY button pinned to the lapel of his jacket, Buford sat down at the young insurance agent's desk.

Joe Bob, Jr. had once worn a Bailey Ballers uniform donated in support of a teenaged baseball team. Through the years afterward he had been an enthusiastic campaign volunteer, handing out VOTE FOR BAILEY buttons and printed flyers for multiple elections. The now thirty-something up-and-comer struck him as a version of his own prior self, almost like the son he had never had: former Boy Scout… currently a solid citizen…smart…hard working…ambitious…

"Joe Bob, I've been thinking about retiring," he said, "and have decided that you are the person most deserving to be entrusted with preserving and protecting the Bailey family legacy. Congratulations."

"Sorry, Mayor Bailey. The boss doesn't allow agency employees to actively take part in politics that have become so divisive. And I really don't have time to hand out buttons and flyers."

"No, no, young man. I'm not talking about the Bailey family political legacy. I've decided to hand over to you the helm…or rather, the keys to the Bailey Insurance Agency. Just keep the lights on, heh, heh, pay the routine operating expenses, assume any liabilities, tend to policy renewals and keep all the profits for yourself. It's a bird's nest on the ground, my boy, and I'm happy to pass along to you on a silver, uh, platter the, uh, opportunity that was handed down to me."

"Gee, thanks, but no thanks," said the spoiled young upstart, a typical product of his generation's inbred sense of entitlement. "I hope to someday have my own business, but want to earn my own way, starting with a clean slate not encumbered by someone else's, uh, legacy."

Disgusted that the intended beneficiary of his generosity would look a gift horse in the mouth—and shirk the attendant responsibilities of dealing with a few potentially bad teeth, so to speak—Buford retreated from the Allstate office occupied by the newly wily "B'rer Bear".

Trudging warily back toward his besieged office, he silently cursed his misfortune. For him, there would be no memorial statue, no park that continued to bear his name. His legacy would be left-over liabilities for unmet responsibilities foisted upon him by birth with a spoon.

CHAPTER EIGHT

Back at his workstation desk after lunch and an errand, Max Googled for information. To professionally wrap up, not "pad" a report on *Case of the Cat's Mother* that might otherwise make the lay look like a simple matter of just getting a U.S. birth certificate for the client…

On his laptop screen, he read that almost all countries that recognized so-called birthright citizenship were former European colonies—almost all the Spanish-speaking ones—located in the western hemisphere. No European countries recognized unconditional citizenship by *jus soli*—"right of soil"—based on place of birth, as opposed to citizenship *jus sanguinis*—"right of blood"—passed on as parental legacy in other nations, including those in lands of burning sun…

Hmmm.

Regarding Saudi Arabia, he read that citizenship only by inheritance was the rule, but could be revoked if a Saudi obtained citizenship in another country, or— as in the case of Osama Bin Laden—if a citizen became a dissident or terrorist.

Hmmm.

He clicked a link, and onto the screen came the face of Fox News jabberer, Sean Hannity, saying…

"In addition to ongoing deportation of foreign thugs, more good news: lamebrain drain looks to be on the rise. While numerous left-wing Hollywood celebrities have threatened—or should I say promised—to go into exile if an election didn't come out their way, usually they shut up and stay put after calculating the value of their God-given American citizenship.

"Yeah, the meows of Kim K, Amy Schumer, Barbra, Cher, Whoopi, and of course Jane Fonda have proven to be more catty than their bites. But not the howling of druggie rock star, Courtney Love, who has announced her decision to follow Ellen Degeneres and Rosie O'Donnell, both of whom have already walked the plank in reaction to President Trump's re-election.

"Unlike other famous grousers, Courtney, Ellen and Rosie must not have consulted with their lawyers, who would have advised them that when Facebook co-founder, Eduardo Saverin, chose to renounce his U.S. citizenship in favor of a tax-friendly foreign haven, Uncle Sam slapped an exit tax of the value on his holdings acquired as an American. I know, I know, getting rid of them and the other three stooges — Barbra, Cher and Whoopi — would be among multiple good reasons to repeal the tax.

"But in defense of lamebrains who came along after high schools stopped teaching Civics, most current American citizens have probably never even heard of the book that used to be required reading: *A Man Without a Country*, that tells the story of a young U.S. Army Lieutenant, Phillip Nolan, who in the early 1800s was put on trial with Aaron Burr for treason, and famously shouted: 'Damn the United States! I wish I may never hear of the United States again!'"

Neither had Max ever heard of the joker, who — according to Hannity — got his wish by being sentenced to exile aboard U.S. Navy warships. For the rest of his life Nolan lived as a prisoner on high seas…transferred regularly from ship to ship… never allowed to set foot in home port…never provided any information about events in his homeland…until beseeching a young sailor to not make the same mistake, and saying:

"Remember, boy, that behind officers and government, and people, there is the Country Herself, your country; and that you belong to her as you would belong to your own mother. Stand by her, boy, as you would stand by your mother!'

"And while some Hollywood lefties and others cheapen their own precious gift of American citizenship by renouncing it, their Blue State comrades have got lower court lefty judges to block President Trump's Executive Order putting an end the harebrained notion that citizenship automatically goes to offspring of foreigners who happen to get born within United States borders."

Executive Order? Uh oh, there went the client's claim to being an American, and along with it a thousad-dollar fee to Yours Truly.

"Not to worry," said Hannity. "Though it will likely take prolonged judicial process, the U.S. Supreme Court is bound to uphold the Trump Order on its legal merits and importance to national security."

Max tentatively sighed in tentative relief.

"But hey, you don't have to take my word," said the famous Fox News commentator, swiveling his square head to face an old man beside him. "Here to document the perils of so-called 'birthright citizenship' is Dr. William Steele, whose 1958 high school Senior Paper—self-published later under the title *Anchor Babies Aweigh*—went largely unheeded until recently. What's up, Doc?"

"Chinese penises, to put it bluntly," said the expert. "The Fourteenth Amendment provides, quote: 'All persons born or naturalized in the United States ...'"

"And are, quote, 'subject to the jurisdiction thereof, are citizens of the United States'," said the talkative cable news show host. " Lefties ignore the jurisdiction clause as though it didn't exist."

"Well, yes, even before the Fourteenth Amendment was ratified, the Civil Rights Act of 1868 more clearly expressed, quote..."

"Expressed, quote: 'All persons born in the United States, and not subject to any foreign power' would be considered citizens," said Hannity. "And the later Supreme Court decision in *Elk v. Wilkins*, Justices denied American citizenship of an American Indian because he 'owed immediate allegiance to' his tribe or nation', and not the United States. It took the Indian Citizenship Act of 1924 to correct that miscarriage of law, which would not have been necessary if the Fourteenth Amendment meant what the lefties say."

"Well, yes, but the issue became largely political after the Court..."

"Yeah, Democrats cite the loosely broad language in the 1898 case of *U.S. v. Kim Ark* to support the lamebrained notion of 'birthright by soil', even though the case involved citizenship of a child born to lawful, permanent U.S. residents. It's a hell of a reach from there to saying that a kid born to Venezuelan gangbangers, here illegally, has to be accepted as an American kid-next-door."

"Well, yes, as I say, while the status of so-called 'anchor babies' was once thought of ..."

"Tell my viewers, Dr. Steele. While the problem used to be seen in terms of costs to taxpayers of shelling out freebies to Mexicans, then became a crisis of foreign gangbangers importing fentanyl and violence along with themselves, now..."

"Now it's a grave issue of national security, Mr. Hannity, which I flew all the way from Arizona to explain. You see, so-called 'citizenship tourism' has morphed into..."

"Yeah, the Chinese are exporting sperm-and-eggs like a greasy-spoon diner, paying big bucks to surrogate American mothers to hatch 'American-by-birthright' offspring, then taking the little Commies to their mainland with plans to..."

"It's my book, damnit, and yes, the 'subject to the jurisdiction thereof' clause of the Fourteenth Amendment is, at the very least, ripe for fundamental interpretation and clarification by the Supreme Court."

"Again, not to worry, Doc. With the kibosh put on so-called 'birthright citizenship' by Trump approved by the Supreme Court, grown-up Chinese anchor babies trying to invade the United States of America will be turned 'aweigh' by Uncle Sam for good."

Hmmm.

While a thousand-dollar fee was still to be had for, okay, possibly short-term Ahab the Arab citizenship by so-called birthright, Max Googled "How to obtain an Oklahoma birth certificate?"

CHAPTER NINE

♫The meat in the Army/ They say its's mighty fine/ Last night we had ten puppies/ Today we had just nine...♫

With a playlist of semi-musical marching cadences blasting through earbuds, G.I. Porter took off her welder's mask...clocked out at the metalworks plant that employed her...climbed into her battered old camo-colored Hummer plastered with patriotic LOVE IT OR LEAVE IT bumper stickers...and set out on a mission in Operation Stop Stolen Valor.

♫Biscuits in the Army/ They say are mighty fine/ One rolled off a table/ And killed a buddy of mine...♫

Military service was a Porter family tradition dating back to at least her grandaddy's service in World War II, followed by her daddy's stint in Viet Nam, and culminating with her own combat tours in Iraq and Afghanistan. Yeah, "culminating". She, an only child and childless, was the last of the Porter line, charged with the ongoing obligation to protect and preserve the family heritage.

♫The coffee in the Army/ They say is mighty fine/ It's good for cuts and bruises/ And tastes like iodine...♫

G.I. found a West Main Street parking spot...got out of the Hummer...and hustled into Willie's "Spoils-of-War"Warehouse, the town's excuse for an Army surplus store. Inside, she passed by a section devoted to equipment and supplies related to lawn maintenance, and... Ahhh, enveloped in a glow of olive drab and still familiar aromas...In the words of her daddy's hero, Colonel Kilgore, G.I.—figuratively speaking—"loved the smell of napalm in the morning!"

Admittedly a geardo, she relished the look and feel of discarded rifles, sidearms, bayonets, machetes and knives on display…uniforms, belts, buckles, holstered canteens, hats, caps… a first aid kit…a kevlar helmet…an armored vest called "Chicken Plates"…and of course racks of combat fatigues such as she still always wore. Grenades, though now probably dummies, evoked the kind of nostalgic feelings other people associated with childhood toys.

And since she was there…G.I. commenced to fill a shopping basket with groceries: surplus rations of various dehydrated meats sealed in brown paper sometimes referred to broadly as shit-on-a-shingle…a few easily stowed-and-carried smaller packets labelled "Iron Rations" for emergency consumption as last resorts…tins of meat identifiers: cranberry sauce for turkey, applesauce for pork chops…two sacks of gedunk a/k/a chips and candy…a "First Strike" ration for use in combat or while moving…and a specialized energy bar called Soldier Fuel…

"What brings you by during middle of a weekday, Trans?" said Willie Jackson, the store owner, decked-out in a Marine dress-blue uniform splattered with a salad of campaign ribbons and medals. "Planning a family dinner to celebrate a special occasion?"

"Negatory, Jackson, the old man is still off his feed," she answered, moving back to the hard goods section. Her daddy had developed a preference for civilian food in his older years.

After finding what she'd come for and paying the tab, G.I. noted with suspicion a middle-aged civilian studying a display of unit insignias, campaign ribbons, decorations and medals set between two American flags. If not on a mission, she would have got in the shopper's face and demanded documentation entitling him to purchase—no doubt with intent to claim as his—a puffed-up chestful of signifiers of service and valor earned by others.

Back in the Hummer, an old anti-war song…

♫ *Some folks are born to wave the flag/ They're red, white and blue/ And when the band plays "Hail to the Chief"/ They point the cannon at you...* ♫

Until serving in combat herself, G.I. had not fully understood why her daddy so hated the song about service, and non-service in the Viet Nam War that he fought.

♫*It ain't me, it ain't me/ I ain't no senator's son...* ♫

The Stolen Valor Act of 2005 — making it a crime for a person to fraudulently claim receipt of a valor award — was struck down by the Supreme Court on grounds of violating pseudo patriots' rights of free speech. A new statute partially correcting the constitutional flaw by limiting prosecution to thefts of valor for profit was enacted in 2013, no doubt with the vote of at least one of at least five modern-day U.S. Senators caught making false claims of having served in military combat: namely, Senator Sidney Blumenthal from Connecticut.

♫*It ain't me, it ain't me/ I ain't no fortunate one...* ♫

Arrived on the front line of Operation Stop Stolen Valor — an unimposing one-story, windowless brick building a few blocks north of downtown — "Geronimo!"

G.I. exited the Hummer...adjusted her black VFW cap, and — armed with the "weapon" she had picked up at Willie Jackson's "Spoils of War" outlet — marched into the local headquarters of the patriotic organization dedicated to U.S military veterans who had served in theaters of combat.

Inside, a meeting of light-blue capped members of the VFW Auxiliary was in progress.

"Sorry, Sergeant-at-the-Guard," said the group's fussy Conductress, the hairdresser, Barbara Felix. "The Auxiliary has reserved the Hall for exclusive use today. And we are in the process of voting on admission of new members."

"As a bona fide veteran of a foreign war and VFW officer, it is my duty to object to Auxiliary membership of Max Morgan."

"This is highly irregular procedure, Sergeant-at-the-Guard Porter. Max Morgan has filed the paperwork documenting that his father, Sergeant Homer Morgan served..."

"Let her speak!" someone shouted.

G.I. reported that her daddy and Max Morgan's old man had

graduated high school together in 1963...had been drafted into the U.S. Army at the same time...and had both been sent to Fort Polk in Louisiana for Basic Training. Morgan, a suck-up, had been regularly assigned to cushy Kitchen Patrol duty, while her daddy had been regularly punished for his "combative attitude" by assignments to Latrine Patrol.

"Well, someone has to care about hygiene," said Felix. "And I must say that someone is shirking the duty here at the hall. Last week, your Judge Advocate, Roger Madison, defiled hall toilets by... Well, let's not talk about that. As I say, Max Morgan has submitted his father's military paperwork, documenting service in the U.S. Army from 1964 to 1966—which was during the Viet Nam War—and was honorably discharged. In addition, he supplemented his application earlier today by donating to VFW Archives this service sidearm worn by his father."

"Only officers, MPs and soldiers in non-combat area wear sidearms," G.I. pointed out, reaching into a Willie's Warehouse brown paper bag. "My daddy returned from combat in Nam with a piece of shrapnel lodged inside his head, which I am sure he would be happy to donate..."

"At the appropriate time and place, after a thorough cleaning, we will consider accepting the, uh, memento , Sergeant-at-the-Guard. In the meantime, however..."

"For loading up the Fort Polk officers mess with heavily-buttered and over-sugared fare, Morgan became the Commanding Officer's pet. He was held over to cook at Fort Polk for the entire two years of his stint. The only 'weapon' he carried, and only legitimate 'memento' of his service, would be this!" G.I. proclaimed, holding up a large Army surplus cook's spoon.

Ohhhhh the Auxiliary members moaned.

Obviously appalled—though the spoon was now free of grease—the Conductress would have been compelled to conduct a vote against Max Morgan membership, but...

"Sorry to interrupt, ladies," said the town's longtime Mayor, Buford "Booster" Bailey, barging into the hall. "In view of the shabby treatment being afforded, or rather, not afforded to veterans, I hereby donate my family's insurance agency—free of charge—to the VFW, for the exclusive benefit of military personnel and their families, sorta like advertised by the *Geico* lizard on tv."

Ohhhhh, the assemblage of mostly split-tails swooned.

"That is most generous of you, Mayor Bailey. I'm sure I speak for the entire VFW Auxiliary membership when I say…"

"If Bailey bails out, who would run the veterans insurance business?" someone asked.

"Max Morgan is a Notary Public who would be good at handling paperwork," someone else proposed.

"Morgan is almost a next-best-thing to a vet."

Hooah! all the Auxiliary members exclaimed in cowardly submission to the blatant subversion of rules for prevention of stolen valor.

In disgust, G.I. executed a crisp about-face and marched from the VFW Hall.

♫*Some folks are born, silver spoon in hand/ But it ain't me, it ain't me/ I ain't no military son, Son…* ♫

CHAPTER TEN

♫*Laughing, laughing, laughing/ Always, always laughing/ In the U.S. Army/ You'll have a helluva howl...* ♫

Max pushed aside a plate of his mom's meatloaf, usually one of his favorites. Up from the kitchen table, he commenced to pace. It was past four-o'-clock. The VFW Auxiliary membership meeting would be over by now. Initiation of new members was scheduled for six-o-clock, and he'd received neither an invitation nor official notice of the festive affair.

"Your father came home from Fort Polk infested with lice," said Mom, who seemed to be almost rooting against him being invited to join the fun. "It took months of lousing to put him right. And from what I hear, that VFW Hall is as lousy as a trench."

♫*Boozing, boozing, boozing/ Always, always boozing/ In the U.S. Army...* ♫

"From what I also hear, there's a lot of drinking and carrying on that goes on at that VFW hang-out," said Mom, "and no doubt other unseemly activity. Your father, a tee-totaler, spent his entire two years of military service on Kitchen Patrol. Cooking night and day for an officers mess, he gained weight and developed high cholesterol. I blame the Army for his obese condition that contributed to his death a few years later by electrical shock."

Max himself was on the verge of blaming his mom, not for his father's demise, but for possibly offending...

Hmmm.

Mom had recently changed insurance companies and put up a yard sign in support of Mayor Bailey's opponent in an upcoming election run-off.

Hmmm.

Was Bailey a VFW Auxiliary member? If so—with His Honor's nose out of joint—he might have blackballed Yours Truly in retaliation.

♫*Grousing, grousing, grousing/ Always, always grousing/ Grousing about the rations/ Grousing about ...* ♫

Dang it, having attended functions at the VFW Hall as a guest, he pictured a jolly band of buddies, already gathered at the bar...drinking root beer...singing old army barrack-room songs and...

Buzz. Buzz. Buzz.

It was Ahab the Arab calling, no doubt anxious to get Yours Truly's report on his citizenship status, but...

"Sorry, Ahab, I'm waiting for an important personal message that might be delivered by important personal messenger. You'll have to come inside."

Minutes passed and...

Knock. Knock. Knock.

...in came the client.

With Mom giving the uncaring son of the local Carlita Somebody a stink-eye...

"Good news, and bad news, Ahab. As it turns out, you're currently a bona fide U.S. citizen just for being hatched on American soil. But President Trump..."

"I know all about such camel shit, and don't trust Trump or your Supreme Court. I hired you, a *notario publico*, to prove the Qareen was an illegal alien in this land from, say, Venezuela. My family's solicitors will take the matter of my citizenship from there."

The ungrateful client went on to say that his father, a *jihadi*, had been expelled from his homeland of Saudi Arabia for holy activities committed in the United States and elsewhere. He himself had renounced his own Saudi citizenship, but...

"That was risky business on your part," said Max. "You could end up like Lieutenant Phillip Nolan, a man without a country, condemned to being kept at sea and unable to enjoy…"

"I have a yacht, Mr. Morgan. I'm almost always cruising from port to port. What I 'enjoy' is being stateless. But your infernal government—in the words of The Sheik's manifesto directed to the American people—continues to rule over others, not by Sharia of Islam and its Constitution and Laws, but by choosing to invent your own laws as you will and desire.

"Damn the United States! I wish I may never hear of the United States again!"

"Dang it, that sounds unAmerican, Ahab. If you feel that way, why…?"

"I ardently desire to be unAmerican by non-inheritance, you idiot! But your government uses its own twisted law to impose citizenship, not based on, but to establish jurisdiction."

"Shame on you, Ishmael Ben Ahab!" said Mom, before marching out of the living room in a huff.

Obviously having studied the matter with the aid of high-powered lawyers, the unhappy client…

"The main body of your Constitution is silent on what establishes citizenship. Without Constitutional provision, however, when—for instance—U.S. citizens 'hatch' offspring while abroad, your government readily accepts the children as citizens by inheritance and presumed allegiance. Others are accepted as citizens by so-called naturalization requiring sworn allegiance.

"The so-called 'Citizenship Clause' added by the so-called Fourteenth Amendment, yes, says 'all persons born in this country, and subject to its jurisdiction are U.S. citizens. But those words are one of five Amendment clauses, all about making adjustments necessitated by the outcome of your civil war. It did not broadly provide for citizenship…not to free white people already living here for almost a century at the time…not to lawmakers who enacted the Amendment and had to already be citizens to be elected. The notion that they would have felt a need to provide citizenship to themselves—and retroactively to George Washington—is absurd."

Hmmm.

"The obvious purpose of the first clause of the Amendment was to provide citizenship to descendants of the African people you had previously brought to these shores as slaves: people who were physically here and 'subject to your government's jurisdiction'."

"So what's your beef, Ahab?"

"I have nothing to do with beef. What 'gets my goat' is that if your government found out I was birthed by a U.S. citizen, it would no doubt use my alleged U.S. citizenship in an attempt to impose jurisdiction over me for purposes of taxation and litigation of other, uh, liabilities."

Huh! Yours Truly's client was an unpatriotic 'Rosie O'Donnell'," Max realized.

"Hey, Buster, maybe you should pull a 'Nolan'. Renounce U.S. citizenship, keep your lousy petro bucks, get on your yacht and…"

"You, a *notario publico*, advise me to admit the false accusation in order to renounce its effect in a tedious process your government would endlessly prolong at my risk and expense? What a fool!"

As Max struggled to get a grip on the unexpected switcheroo in *Case of the Cat's Mother*, a twist implying that Yours Truly had been taking part in a reverse "Anchor Baby" scam…

Knock. Knock. Knock.

He loosened his grip, hotfooted to the front door, opened it, and — Praise the Lord — there stood Ms. Felix. He'd lobbied the VFW Auxiliary Conductress by donating …

"Mr. Morgan, I regret to inform you that the VFW's Sergeant-at-the-Guard Porter has withdrawn her renunciation of membership and agreed to take over management of the former Bailey Insurance Agency for VFW members."

Ah, an unexpected additional benefit of membership.

"Special consideration of your application for VFW Auxiliary membership was therefore not warranted."

Special consideration? Dang, that would have been an honor, but …

"And otherwise, on the merits of the matter, given that the

documentation suggests that your late father served entirely on Kitchen Patrol…"

Max poofed up his chest.

"…as a cook…"

"They say an army moves on its stomach, not is feet. Heh, heh."

"… not in a war, campaign, or expedition on foreign soil or in hostile waters or in air above—but in the kitchen of an officers mess at Fort Polk, Louisiana."

Uh oh.

Max's dander rose as the Conductress handed back his father's U.S. Army service revolver—but not the box of chocolates he'd also donated.

"Your application to join us by right of inheritance has been denied."

♫*Lousing, lousing, lousing/ Always, always lousing/ Lousing of our private parts/ Lousing of our hair…* ♫

Oh well, from his prior attendances at VFW Hall functions as a guest, he had to admit that his mom—like almost always—was right. The premises—in particular, the Men's restroom—were in dire need of "delousing", to put it mildly. And VFW members were, in fact, more rowdy than jolly.

♫*Grousing, grousing, grousing/ Always, always grousing/ Grousing about the rations/ Grousing about…* ♫

What the heck, if admission to college based on legacy was unAmerican, what was so Yankee Doodle Dandy about membership in the Veterans of Foreign Wars Auxiliary?

THE
END